GIVEN GROUND

The Katharine Bakeless Nason Literary Publication Prizes

The Bakeless Literary Publication Prizes are sponsored by the Bread Loaf Writers' Conference of Middlebury College to support the publication of first books. The manuscripts are selected through an open competition and are published by University Press of New England/ Middlebury College Press.

GIVEN GROUND

ANN PANCAKE

MIDDLEBURY COLLEGE PRESS

Published by University Press of New England • Hanover and London

Middlebury College Press

Published by University Press of New England, Hanover, NH 03755

© 2001 by Ann Pancake

Printed in the United States of America

5 4 3 2 1

Library of Congress Cataloging-in-Publication Data

Pancake, Ann.
  Given ground / Ann Pancake.
    p. cm.
"Katharine Bakeless Nason literary publication prizes."
  ISBN 1–58465–118–0 (alk. paper)
  1. Southern States—Social life and customs—Fiction. 2. Maturation
(Psychology)—Fiction. I. Title.
  PS3616.A36 G58   2001
  813'.6—dc21   2001001472

For the people where I grew up, who taught me what's important in a story.

And for Brad

CONTENTS

ACKNOWLEDGMENTS

"Getting Wood" and "Wappatomaka" originally appeared in *Antietam Review*; "Cash Crop: 1897" in *The Massachusetts Review*; "Jolo" in *Mid-American Review*; "Tall Grass" in *Shenandoah*; "Ghostless" and "Revival" in *The Virginia Quarterly Review*; "Sister" in *Wind*; "Crow Season" in *The Chattahoochee Review*; "Redneck Boys" in *Glimmer Train Stories*; "Bait" in *Sundog*; and "Dirt" in *The Chariton Review*.

The author would also like to thank the National Endowment for the Arts for its support. Deepest gratitude to Brad Comann and Melissa Delbridge for their insightful criticism.

GIVEN GROUND

GHOSTLESS

I opened the gap into the pasture, a single strand of bob wire notched in a twist. The cold came high in my chest, but the wind had finally laid and from some distance I could feel the heat off the horse. The hide-odor off the horse, that soily smell he carried even in the winter. I pushed my face into it, into the hollow behind the shoulder, before the belly swell. Old, patient horse. Indifferent horse. Twenty-seven years old, born on my grandfather's farm. Had outlived both him and my daddy now. The dogs sat at the edge of the yard and bayed nothing, just bayed. I turned my cheek to his skin and looked down towards the creek, to the sycamores, ghost trees, bone-shiny in the littlest moon.

My daddy had said just put him under a big tree.

Inside there was more food than I'd ever seen on our table, and fat women in print dresses perched on the couch with saucers balanced cross their knees, while their husbands slunk, dangerous-mouthed, from room to room. I found the fried squirrel, floured nice, on its chipped platter. I still had horse on my hands, and I smeared them across my Sunday pants, listening, the wood fire brightening my back.

I

"I hear some of 'em are up in Dayton. Some of her people."

"Yeah, it's John Eddy and them is who it is."

I ate my squirrel, quiet, that good black meat, so tender you could drop it from the bone with your tongue, and the fragile hips.

"Remember John Eddy? The fat one with the cast to his eye."

"No, that was Connie who you're thinking of."

My daddy had shot the squirrels just days before, fox squirrels. I'd helped him dress them out along the creek. He'd come at my head with the knife, and I flinched, but he just nicked off a little swath of hair and laid it beside the squirrel skin. *Look here,* he said. *You're colored like that squirrel is.*

"Better for the boy."

"Got better schools up there in Dayton."

Outside the dogs were still barking, the chops falling even and deliberate, and I knew they would be at it all night.

"With a dog chain," one of them said again. I watched him shake his head. My daddy had looked uneasy in his box, his legs drawn out straight and him touching his heart.

"Be still now. The boy's right there by the fire."

* * *

Those last years before we left the land were dry ones, the oaks making naught but the little acorns that dropped in August and burned up on the ground. Then there was no mast for the deer, and hunger-doped by spring they strayed near the house to crop the early grass where the dogs brought them down, the young ones goat-bleating the way they will. Buzzards busy all of March, all of April. Vulture constellations. You could catch wind off them from some far away in the woods, overripe venison rot, and the dogs writhing in the carcasses on their backs.

There were ditches wrapped around those hills, and people said they were left over from the War Between the States. *Don't tell anyone,* my daddy said, *we will have out-of-staters walking the ridges, picking up things the way they do.* One afternoon when I was very small we were rabbit-hunting in a power cut and saw a man across the way. My daddy yelled at him, but he wouldn't turn. And we followed him, him plodding tired and steady through that parched brush, making no effort to get ahead of us nor none to wait, and we came up on him and called again, and that time he looked at us. My daddy grabbed hold my shoulder, stopped, and let the other one go. Gray, all of one color he was, with the electric wires crackling over his cap.

That night my daddy came in my room and sat the edge of my bed with his back to me, his long-john shirt whitening a space in the dark. He told me that had been no man at all, but a ghost, a Confederate soldier, and I stiffened in my iron bed. Here was thick with ghosts, he told me, and told me not to be afraid, but I was, that the first one I ever saw and me maybe four years old. After he left I cried with the blanket up over my head, listening for those ghost boots slapping up the stairs. Here was thick with ghosts as it was with deer, my daddy told me, all of them pushed in from the outside. *Think,* he told me. *There's no place else for them to go.*

* * *

Some days my daddy wanted to be alone. He filled his jacket pockets with venison jerky strung on greasy twine, and he left before light, penning the dogs in the house behind him because he didn't want them following him and couldn't bear to see them chained. I'd wake with a wet nose in my face, the other dog snuffling the corners, and puddles on the floor. The odor of gun oil in the kitchen and the notches along the table rim where he'd whittle, nervous, as he finished his breakfast with his left hand.

My mother'd tell me wipe up the puddles, her dressing rapid while the coffee made because we would be going to town now, and she uncoiled the pantyhose over her legs with both hands, the cigarette bobbing on her lower lip. She waited tables at the Stonewall Jackson and didn't like to see a boy idle, made me stack the little sugar packs in their wire cages and fill the creamers. The locals would get in early, Bud and Mr. Haines, and Twink and the rest of them. They sat with me at the counter over pancakes and asked without looking in my face, "How's your daddy?"

"Boy don't say much, does he?"

"Shy," my mother'd tell them.

The Stonewall was the only restaurant in town, and after nine on weekends the out-of-staters stopped, passing through to their skiing or their second homes. They locked their car doors behind them, suspicious in their bright loud jackets and pants. Wouldn't nobody accidentally shoot them wearing those kind of clothes, Twink would make a joke, but it wasn't accidents they were worried about, said Mr. Haines. Bud didn't even have to look up, could tell it was them by how hurried they opened the door. "Here come the imports," he'd say. They complained about the cigarette smoke and the grease on the bacon. Their health was important. My mother carried the bacon back to the kitchen and sopped at it with paper towels. I sat on my stool, drawing pictures on the back of used placemats, trees, and twelve-point bucks. "How's Hector?" Mr. Haines asked my mother.

She would sigh, "Ohh, all right."

Once one of the imports took my picture even though there was nothing to see, just me sitting at the side of the building on a bread rack because I couldn't bear any longer to be inside. Foreigners. From-away-from-here. They talked like people on TV, that whitewashed talk of people from no place.

* * *

Ghost-dogged my daddy was, saw them the way some people can spy the last berries in the brier roar of a thicket or brook trout in a root shadow. By the time he was grown and I came along it was in him so keen I couldn't help but catch it. Hunting or woodcutting we'd carry a lunch and eat in the house rubble way up those little draws, us resting on the crumpled chimbley stones, all that was left of the old people a stubborn shock of jonquils, maybe, a buckled sheet of stove iron. Runty deer picking their way past, they were rank as weeds back in there. They'd freeze up and stare at us, confused, until they winded us and arched away. Then my daddy would catch sight of a ghost. I could smell it off him like an animal hide, and I'd watch, too, even though I didn't want to, and a shape would come. Like comes the body of a black snake from a black limb, a shape would come.

The first time, he told me, he'd been just a little boy clearing grass in the big orchard up on Twelve Square, him working with a made-over boy-size scythe, ticking up and down the rows. This was when my grandaddy was a landowner and hired a dozen men in the summers, sweet corn in the bottoms, apples on those limestone ridges. My daddy caught his ankle with the blade one morning a good ways off from the others, and while he bled into the timothy, a man gathered himself from the grass. *Gathered himself out*

5

the grass, I mean all of the pieces fell like they were spilling one at a time out some kind of opening and feeling for each other, for how they fit together, you see. He was a big strong man, ground-colored like a deer, and he was taken with the little scythe. He picked it up, the blood already dry on it, and he looked at his quarter-moon reflection there. By the time the workers found my daddy, the man had pulled himself back through his rift.

Sometimes he'd make me sit for hours. On a log without moving for so long I thought I could feel the world drift under my feet while we waited to see who would come. When he was a boy it was different, my daddy would whisper at me between his teeth, the deer scarcer and stronger and barrel-bellied with the heavy racks. The ghosts different as well, and less common than they were now. When he was a boy sitting a watch, he would see old-timers pass out of a gap and clip along the flanks of the hills with wild gobblers slung over their backs, running those deer paths like the slant was level ground, *like they were born to it,* my daddy said. And then sometimes he'd take the safety off and make me do it the way the old-timers had. I ran with the gun carried crosswise in my hands, one on the stock, the other under the barrel, dancing on the edges of my feet the deer ruts strung sideways along those steep ridges. Juggling the rifle like eggs, my chest heaving, I could see the black space behind my eyes where I knew I would go if I fell. *That's the way you do it,* my daddy called from behind. *Don't be scared.*

By the time I was born it was different. The little land we'd held on to went unplowed, pushing up the only crops Uncle Sam would pay for, set-aside, waste stuff, cockaburrs and thistles and rabbit tobacco. Government crops. Up in the mountains the springs drew back into the ground, and it was just tiny deer prints scoring the mud they left behind. The ghosts we saw were ragged old people, lots of them, clambering up the gullies, ribby like the deer and dry-apple-faced, clambering empty-handed up the banks and always fading back into the dead leaves before they reached the bench. And the Confederates, again and again, the Confederates, all the time watching the ground under their feet. We saw one in nothing but a horse blanket and his boots. Down, down under the mountain the traffic made a wind sound.

Some days we didn't go up there at all but sat along the creek instead, on the warm rocks there, and he watched the humped hills beyond the sycamores and told a story for every wrinkle, a buck he'd shot there, a bobcat he saw fifteen years earlier, the ghost of a club-footed girl. *Put it in your head,* he'd say, *you have a good memory.* He'd rap me above my ear with his knuckles, just hard enough so it hurt, and I put it there. I could close my eyes and unroll the whole range in my mind, every fold, every rise, the color of every season. *Think,* he'd tell me, speaking of the deer and the ghosts again, *there's nowhere else for them to go. And what about this?* he told me. *Finally they'll all be pushed onto one acre of ground, and then what?* He tore deer jerky off the string with his teeth and rolled white store-bought bread into gray pellets between his palms.

* * *

The bottom grew second homes that looked more alike than corn plants did. Among them sagged the house where my daddy was born, a ghost itself in the middle of all that aluminum siding, the house vine-swallowed and collapsing in on itself as though it had drawn a single deep breath then never let it go. Foreclosed, I knew from listening at the Stonewall, "fore" like "for sale" and the "closed" spoke for itself. Even I could read the "No Trespassing" sign, but he said that didn't mean us, and when I seized up in that thistly yard, ghost-scared about the place, he grabbed my arm and jerked me over the porch. The plaster had shaken loose of the walls, showing logs like house ribs underneath, and the honeysuckle runners through the kitchen windows. Swallows in there, and wasps and mud daubers, the furniture carrying a crust. Snakes and groundhogs denned up under the floors.

Then he told me go upstairs, to make sure. He said the steps wouldn't hold him. *Go on up,* he said, *see what's up there.* I shook my head. *Get up there,* he said. I stood quiet in the spoke wreck of the banister on the floor. *You heard me.* He wasn't carrying his gun that day, but he had his deerknife. The one that opened them between the breastbone, snick, easy like that. He pulled it out. *Do you love your daddy?* he asked.

I climbed. I climbed them careful because they were punky and bowed in the middle, and I stopped on the landing. I could hear my daddy breathing heavy down below me. I crooked my neck to see what was ahead up there in the hall, and the blood came loud in my ears, it came whum, whum, whum. *Get on,* he hissed. The hallway lay empty in front of me, the stink of the rat dirt and the mote pools, dreamy. All my skin rose up and the whumming so loud now I heard nothing else, but I knew he was down there listening for my feet. I started walking. The door to each room was either open or gone and I peeked sidewise into each one expecting to see it. And each one was empty, emptier than the rooms downstairs. Just the water stains making pictures on the wallpaper and beyond the window panes, the vines and then the second homes.

I walked the hall to the end. The last door was shut. I knew that was where it would be.

I reached out and eased the door open with my boot toe. It swung in. In the middle of the floor lay a heap of olive-colored cloth. I forced myself in and turned it over with my foot, keeping my body as far away as I could, expecting a face to roil up out of it. But they were empty work clothes, soiled with rat droppings.

I walked all the way back along that hall, ghostless. "Nothing up here, Daddy," I called from the top of the steps. I heard him leave, bolting the front door behind him. By the time I crawled out the window and onto the porch, he was across the field and halfway to the road, a long brown twist, wind-driven in jerks along the thistled ground.

* * *

I sat my stool in the Stonewall Jackson drawing deer with a ballpoint pen, my mother hazy beside me in her cigarette break, mid-morning and no customers but a pair of out-of-staters whispering secretly at a corner table. The door opened behind us and somebody called out "Mona!" like he was surprised to see her there. "How you been?" He creaked like horse tack, straddling the stool on the other side of her, and I knew it was the sheriff.

"Ohh, all right," she said.

He spoke of the cold and the dry and of business. He shouted at Minxie who owned the place and sat in the back listening to gospel while he ate his toast and honey there beside the deep fryer, hollered at Minxie that he'd heard the McDonald's was finally on its way, ha, ha. I had a big buck all finished and filled in the bullets flying at his head.

"Listen," the sheriff finally said. "They've been complaining about Hector. The people in the bottom."

My mother said nothing.

"Trespassing, but that's not all. Poaching, too."

9

She crushed a butt in the Kool ashtray.

"I just wanted to tell you," the sheriff said. "Before I have to do something. You know."

She didn't speak.

"Not that I want to do something. But you know how it is," he said.

"You want some coffee?" my mother said.

*   *   *

He started fooling all the time in the woodshed saying he was building something, but he wasn't. He told me stay out which meant I didn't have to carry logs in, that was fine. I pulled up against a knothole, the woodshed soft and raincolored even in the dry, and I let my eye open to the dark. He sat there on a stovelength handling the dog chain. I looked over my shoulder at the dogs down in the leafless forsythia along the house walls, bundled in on themselves against the cold.

"Kit!" my mother yelled from the back door. "Kit!" She told me to pick up sticks in the yard. There had been a high wind the night before and she didn't like to see me idle. Afraid I'd come up lazy like my daddy. Lazy, crazy, like my daddy, I felt the rhyme with the sides of my tongue. I dumped the sticks in the pasture where the old horse stood with his rump to the air and rolled one muddy eye at me. Dry winter wind, no moisture in it. I could see my mother in the kitchen window, watching. She hated this place even though she was of it.

I went inside to warm up. She fried deer liver and onions in an iron skillet. "Go get your daddy to eat," she said.

"I'm not allowed in there," I said.

"I said go get your daddy," she said.

"Daddy!" I called from outside the shed. "Daddy, come

and eat!" We had nailed hides on the wall of the shed to cure, and under the eaves we'd hung the puny racks of the deer we'd shot in past years. Splayed out muskrats and coons, eyeless, snoutless, watching me through the holes in their faces, and the deer skulls above, watching. Animal bones on the outside the woodshed, I thought, and tree bones in. Bones, bones, bones. Oh, it was airy. I could hear a big limb up the mountain snap.

I told my mother he wouldn't come out. She threw the fork on the stove and slammed out the door, coatless.

The liver and onions burned up in the pan.

*　*　*

My daddy said he wouldn't be buried in no square. He said just lay him up the mountain under a big tree, but they put him in a cemetery boxed with a picket fence. It was tipped with one strand of bob wire to keep out the stock. I've seen no ghosts since.

In a city, I can tell you, it is all straights and angles, your eye broken up by corners and by edges. Your eyes are never rolled the way the hills do back there. Nothing back home wide open, it is true, but nothing sharp, all the time easy on your eyes. And when you stand between the ridges, your heart beat stops right there and drums along the sides. It is not like here where there is nothing to dam the throb. Here where it spreads flat and thin forever.

Sometimes on the stoop of an evening or during a break at work over a cigarette, I close my eyes and try to unfold it the way he told me I could have it in my head. But I can no longer make it come.

I can make nothing come but this. The feel of the earth under my back, my knees. The smell of the heat in a rock.

REVIVAL

When they hear the ambulance groveling out of the creek-bed, her mother moves to the window over the sink and braces herself on the heels of her hands. The panic that's stoved down inside her borne on the brace of her hands, but none of it showing except in her eyes. The eyes slipping, starting, as though anxious to get out of her head.

The old man's feeding hand quits. He hovers, too, featureless under the brim of his hat, ear cocked to the engine—there are no sirens—of what he still calls an "emergency car." Lindy looks away from her father's lunch. Leftover deer spaghetti, the noodles overcooked and the sauce gamey because the worst of the venison they always have ground. The old man shoves back from the table with his red handkerchief still tucked in his pants waist.

"Won't let us come near her, no she won't. No, she won't now. Won't let us anywhere near her. No. She won't." Her mother, murmuring. The ambulance rattles across the low wooden bridge at the foot of the hill, shifts gears, and pulls the rise to the house.

Lindy follows the pair of them into the yard. She doesn't own a winter coat because she lives in a warm place now, but her mother forgets to put hers on. As they wait for Eddie, the EMT, to get out of the ambulance and tell them what happened, Lindy watches her mother's arms mottle pink in the cold.

"I'm real sorry," Eddie says. He shakes his head with his face to the ground. "Can't pick up a heartbeat in the baby. But they won't let us take her out. She needs to get down to the clinic. You all don't want her having it up in there."

Her mother continues, tearless, droney. "She won't let none of us near her. No, deed, she won't. Nowhere near her."

Eddie lifts his face. "How long you in for, Lindy?"

Lindy hasn't seen him since high school graduation. Now he looks more like his father than himself. "Just for Christmas," Lindy says.

"We'll send Lindy up there to talk sense into her," her father decides.

Lindy glances at him, sharp. He stands there ridiculous with the red bandanna aproned under his camouflage jacket. But because she only visits once a year, she can't say too much. She's been expecting it all morning anyway.

She turns back inside, seeking the woodstove. When she got in last night, it had been too dark to see the house good. Now it strikes her. High, narrow, and a scaly white.

*   *   *

Every Christmas Lindy'd stand beside the conveyor belt under electronic monitors with the other passengers, well-dressed and cologned. Behind her, silent and just out of sight, the odor of hunting jacket, of little-washed man, and of the wood smoke he's carried all the way from the house. She knows her father'll try to merge his rust-bitten Chevrolet Citation onto the freeway outside the airport and be forced onto the shoulder before he can snatch his little piece of road. They'll sit across the plastic table under fluorescent lights in Leesburg while he halves a Big Mac with his pocketknife, rinses the blade in a cup of water, and dries it in his handkerchief.

She knows the open four-lane across northern Virginia, not a bump in the hardtop or a lurch in the grade, and the sun putting down, reluctant and pinched, back behind the Blue Ridge. They thread the last little city in the dark. Tunneling. A few miles before the state line, the road chokes to two lanes, and the Citation chatters up the incline and nearly drags to a halt before they crest and hurtle down the other side into where she was born. Only a hundred miles from Washington, D.C., a city she didn't see until she was eighteen years old.

Then she is back, and it comes with a weight. Tunneling. Through those little water gaps with the oak limbs nearly arbored overhead, and the gaunt frame houses, intermittent, strung in puny Christmas lights. Busting into the brief clearings, the barns and hayricks heaving up, now and again, then past, entombed some place behind them, the headlights no more than a glance in this kind of dark. And on both sides the car, the dead brush at her elbows. Dirty blonde and ruffled in the tiny starlight there.

The old man speaks. "Dee-Dee's got some kind of female problems."

"What do you mean?" Lindy asks.

"I don't know. I just been told she's having some kind of problems with her insides."

Lindy studies her reflection in the side window. Against the receding shale bank, her face fixed, transparent.

"How far along is she now?"

"I don't know. Six. Seven months."

* * *

Her mother makes her take two plastic grocery bags. They bulge with home-canned green beans, Christmas sugar cookies, and a butcher-papered chunk of tenderloin, primest part of the deer. To get back in there, she follows a creekbed that runs dry almost every day of the year, a track too rough to carry the Citation. All her mother and the old man will call the father of this baby is "some Shotzhouser boy." They and her sister are not speaking again although they live within three-quarters of a mile and Dee-Dee and the boy are squatting rent free on the old man's land. They're holed up in something more camper than trailer in those timbered-off hills that used to be pasture back when a person could make a living farming up and down land like this. And even though the cattle were long ago sold off, they've spited the ground forever. Each hill corkscrewed with hoof-worn grooves.

Lindy smells snow, something she never smells outside of here. It comes to her hard in the back of her throat like such smells must come to animals. Then she can see the bald with the trailer nubbed out there on it, and she is taken aback by the sudden violence of metal in the rinsed-out winter grass. She climbs the slope, depending on the boy to answer the door and send her away.

There is no screen. She raps on a warped door of that dimpled stuff trailer doors are made of. After a few minutes, it opens a third of the way, and what she sees first is that this Shotzhouser boy is even younger than Dee-Dee, and Dee-Dee is just twenty. He leans out in a plaid flannel shirt hanging open to a naked man's chest with a brand-new look to it, a pureness to it. And this calls up something in Lindy, and suddenly, she remembers. Hard hands. Yellow dirt. The taste of cider turning that they carry in their mouths. She begins to understand what Dee-Dee does.

She stands self-conscious of the winter clothes she's had to borrow—her mother's kerosene-stained coat, plastic old-woman boots—knowing keen that this is not the thing to feel at such a time. "I'm Lindy, Dee-Dee's sister," she says, and waits to be told to get out.

The boy takes his lower lip in his teeth and looks past her. She recalls that his first name may be Shane. "I think I heard a heartbeat," the boy says. He pauses. For the lip to steady, Lindy sees. "Come in and listen."

The trailer is overheated as the Fourth of July. She drops the grocery bags in the dim behind the front door, the only distinct object in the draped room an aquarium of illuminated urine-colored water. From the cramped kitchen, a thin odor of unwashed breakfast dishes. Fried egg yolks gelling on plastic plates. Shane is already disappearing down the narrow hall, and Lindy stumbles after him, into a tiny bedroom that reeks of sweat.

Lindy had expected from Dee-Dee her usual hostility or smugness. She gets neither. She also doesn't get a greeting. Dee-Dee's face rises off the pillow in a knot, drained white with a purplish cast left behind. Red eyes move in the white face like a rabbit's. It's been a long time since Lindy's seen her without makeup, and naked of it, Dee-Dee makes up quick the ten years between herself and Lindy. Shane has her stomach bared, it blown out taut and showing its veins. Dee-Dee waits for her with the boy.

"Put your ear to her belly," Shane whispers. His hair is damp around the edges, his own heartbeat rapid in a vein in his head.

It occurs to Lindy that she hasn't touched her sister's stomach since Dee-Dee was five or six. Outside the single bedroom window crouches that sky, foaming low with snow refusing to fall. Lindy loops her hair behind her ear, inhales, and stoops.

She can feel the heat off Dee-Dee's skin without touching her. Lindy squats there in stupid obedience, in self-disgust. But she is not surprised. Other boys like this one she has given in to, in situations almost as foolish, and way more dangerous. She knows she won't catch a rhythm under Dee-Dee's skin. She doesn't even listen. She concentrates on appearing to listen while not actually touching Dee-Dee's body. After what she figures is long enough, she stands back up.

"Nothing," she says. "Sorry."

"No-o," Shane insists. He stops and swallows. "You got to move your head around. Listen in different places."

"Look, why don't I call the Rescue Squad back and they can take you all on down to the clinic? They got . . . more sensitive instruments down there."

Shane cuts her a look with snakebite in it. When she leaves the bedroom, he tries to slam the door behind her, but flimsy like it is, it makes only a shabby smack.

She finds herself on the heap of cinderblocks that is their front stoop. The block she sits on wobbles. From under the trailer, a white cat skits out, petrifies at the sight of her, then bullets around the back. It shows clear the knobs of its shoulders and hips, and Lindy recalls first moving out of here. Then most of the dogs and cats outside looked fat. Now the ones inside look skinny. That is the difference. She stares at the grimy margarine tub that is the cat's dish, the pork chop bones scattered in the dirt, and cannot think of a thing to do. Everything collapsed again into this single clod of narrow house, spent farm, and the couple miles that encrust them. An intactness not a thing in the world can prick. Not a television, not comings and goings, not births nor deaths, not the twelve years she's spent outside.

Her mother had lost several between Lindy and Dee-Dee. "Your mother's people have always had an easy time getting pregnant, a hard time staying that way," her father would say. The losses had something to do with the distance between the sisters, a distance much greater than age. Dee-Dee is loved three times more, the way Lindy figures it. First, the inevitable love skip down to the youngest; second, the way parent love seems ferti-lized by the ones who make the most trouble; and third, the lost babies before Dee-Dee finally lived, making Dee-Dee precious in a way Lindy never was. But Lindy still carries memories of several. Blood curling over toilet water, a riddle there in the iron-stained bowl. Lindy un-certain whether it came out of a person or the pipes, and both to her at five years old somehow equally sad. An-other time, her father returning from the clinic to tell her a little brother had died. "How come?" Lindy asked. "Well," her father thought. "Because he was no bigger than my thumb." Then he stuck out the thumb to show her, and always Lindy would see it that way. A little thumb baby, legless, armless, a crushed up infant face in place of the nail.

The door opens behind her. She turns. Desperation has forced Shane to forgive her.

"I swear, " Shane says. "I heard it. Can you come back in and listen?"

This time Dee-Dee has her face away, her eyes closed. Lindy kneels and shuts her own and wonders why she didn't do it this way before. So much easier shut eyes make it. Closed up in her head, the odor of anonymous sweat that had hit her when she walked in comes to her as familiar as the snow smell did.

It is family sweat. The smell of how her mother sweats. Of how Lindy herself sweats.

Suddenly, Lindy wants to believe. She wants this bad. She lays her ear on Dee-Dee's bare skin without flinching. She strains to hear the way she would if she'd been listening for that second noise in the night. She stretches her neck, does move her head around, does listen in different places. She even turns her face over in case the other ear might do a better job. And she remembers (she had forgotten, she slips back into the knowing the way her tongue loosens for talking here), she remembers how wrong they have it when they blame these pregnancies on carelessness. When, Lindy remembers, it is the opposite, it is a carefulness, a kind of mindfulness (the absence of anything else to do, to expect, the absolute lack of distraction, until that single person, the anticipation of the next time, dilates universal), a concentration only the very imaginative or the desperate can recover after passing age twenty-two.

Lindy waits. Her breathing patterns Dee-Dee's. But she hears nothing in there but, distant, Dee-Dee's bowels working a little.

Finally, she straightens up with her eyes still closed and shakes her head for the boy. Then she opens them, and her heart socks up between her lungs. She had forgotten the full-length mirrors covering the closet doors across from where she stands. Lindy in the mud-crusted boots, the dirty-pink quilted coat daubed over with kerosene spills, her face rough, chapped, bloodless except in the nose. That raw and red. For several minutes, Lindy has never left out of here at all.

Once she escapes to the yard, she stands with her back against the trailer wall and strains to see distance. She's brought up short by the cattle-racked knob across the creek. The cold beats her breath into the visible, and she jams her scarf to her mouth and bites down, an old, old habit. It returns to her in the taste of damp wool. A time when she was small, must have been seven or eight, she can date it by the wool taste, the strings that tied the cap she was made to wear then. She and the old man, not so old then, not yet blanked in the face then, and her uncle Jerry, and her cousin, Jerry's boy, the one they call Thumper. Them walking their property line above an old orchard of Hebert Stills's, reblazing with a hatchet the healed-over trees that marked their bounds. And as they passed an old cistern on Hebert's side, the concrete ledge of it a little higher than Lindy's head and the whole thing no bigger across than a couple bathtubs, they heard a splashing and wheezing in there. Somehow a little deer had tumbled into it. Her father lifted her up on one of those giant apple crates so she could see down into the cistern, and then the men and Thumper went to fishing it out. But there was no touching it. The little deer, a last-year's fawn, paddling frantic, walled crazy in her eyes. The men prodding at her with boards, and Thumper, scrambled up and clinging like a salamander to the cistern wall, swiping at her with as much arm as he could free without falling, but there was no touching her. She swam away from the old man to Jerry, and away from Jerry to Thumper, over and over in a star. Until she was nearly dead and had no choice. Then they levered her out with the planks, and Uncle Jerry cradled her down to the ground where she lay in a little crumple. Too tired even to shake, to flick, much less to run away.

Lindy realizes that for some minutes there has seeped from behind the trailer wall a muffled murmuring. She drops what is in her mind and pays attention. Faint and unbroken, almost like a television at a distance, but eerier, somehow, than a television.

The sound lures her back up over the rubble of stoop and through the warped front door. It comes from the bedroom. She moves silently over the balding carpet, smells behind her the raw deer haunch she dropped earlier start to cook or to spoil. It's hard to tell which. The bedroom door stands slightly open. Without getting against it, Lindy peers in.

From her angle, Lindy can see Dee-Dee only from her breasts down. Shane has taken off the flannel shirt and has his back to Lindy, but she sees that although he's not listening anymore, his head's bowed so low his bangs drag Dee-Dee's navel. Lindy moves a little at the naked back despite herself. The perfectness of it. How brief it will keep back here.

The singsong throbs along with a heat behind it. Lindy understands that she couldn't tell what it was earlier because Shane is not speaking any words. Still, the contours of the thrum blaze up in her a remembering. A pattern beaten in her nerves. Eighteen years of Sunday mornings and Wednesday nights cramped and resistant in a pew. It is the shell of prayer he chants. A boy who knows the shape of prayer, but has never learned the words.

Lindy shifts to where she can see the front of him in the mirror across the bed. Once again, she feels nearly slapped with how young he is. His breath hovering Dee-Dee's skin. She watches his hand moving over Dee-Dee's stomach, over the dead fetus, in tight circles. Every minute or so, at the same interval in the drone, he uses one finger to trace a little cross on Dee-Dee's skin.

Now it comes to Lindy what Shane's trying to do, and she reels back hard. Finds herself caught short by the hall wall behind her. Groping through the front room, she trips and falls on her knees before she finds the door. She heads up back of the trailer, away from the house, towards the treeless knob. It's beginning to turn dark, but she thinks she can get into that open place first.

JOLO

Jolo.

Say it.

Say _Jolo._

Jolo, Jolo boy (moving).

Moving through air as sticky as the blood that moves inside her, same heat as the blood, the spit inside her, that moves inside, so that there in the dark she forgets where she ends, forgets where her skin stops, her skin does not stop, she is continuous. Moving through the weed smells, all the different green smells, single, then symphonic, single, then symphonic, the river low and mucky, a fertile rotty smell, low low dog days August smell. Not a bad smell, even though it is a just short of shit smell, but the river is not unloved for it, no, actually loved by Connie more tender for it, for its spoiledness, its helplessness, for how people have done it. Moving through the frog and bug burr, the chung, chung, chung, the tiny creature roar, layers of ankles and throats and wings, a sobbing mesh, the sound, too, an extension of her, the sex noise that shirrs the rind of her head, the kernel of her chest, again, Connie not knowing where her body ends, her not knowing again, and *say it. Jolo.* The name carries a kind of wet heat, a back of the mouth under the tongue, a you-know-what-I'm-saying-heat. *You do.* Carried in the syllables themselves. *No,* she wants to say to the cop, *it's not like that,* she tries to say. *Fires are a dry heat,* she says, and *Jolo's wet, just say his name. Jolo.*

But Connie does not tell the cop. When he asks her the question, which triggers what it is to be with Jolo, she does not even think it in segments, in words, like that, but she thinks it all the same, in another way. Thinks it all at once, intuitive, throbbing. But all the same. Cornered in the grocery store lot after closing where she's been hauled in a Ford Fiesta by a neighbor girl who could find nobody else to ride around with that night, and in this parking lot, when the neighbor girl darts across the pavement to whisper with another carload of kids, Connie tries to follow. But the moment she shows herself in the streetlight—hulky, broad-bottomed in terry-cloth shorts—the deputy sheriff shouts her name from where he spies on them in the shadow of the store. He orders Connie over, and when she obeys, seizes her wrists in his sticky fingers without bothering to get out of the car. He pinches her wrists just inside the window where no one else in the lot can see, him cop-smug, encased in his guns and his fat, but the first time he asks her, she only stares at the puddly sundae beside him on the seat. Then he jerks her arms, and her bracelet snaps, beads tumbling into his lap, and Connie shrinks. He asks her again what she knows about Jolo's part in that summer's fires. And still all Connie can answer, and that not even out loud (not what she thinks, but what she knows) is, *Jolo.* Say his name, and you'll know it's not.

Yet Connie doesn't know. She knows no more at that point about Jolo's part in the recent fires than she knows why Jolo has chosen her, this last a daily source of stun.

Although she does understand, a thick, thick knowledge, why she's drawn to him. Jolo boy. With his chest ribbed like corduroy and his melted ear, his stomach and arm skin lit like glare on the river. At first it was a prickle, then a pull. Then like how hard it is to look away when the nurse's needle enters your arm. Then, gradually, Connie learned, and, yes, it was still the skin, the rosebud ear, like a brand-new animal for Connie to handle, but on top of all that, Connie learned.

Connie, on the other hand, is neither disfigured nor desirable. She was born, she knows, with a mild mistake for a face. Her hips and thighs have blossomed enormous, the way the other girls' will, it is true, shortly after high school, but instead of that inspiring sympathy for Connie, it just makes her more ignored. Connie a fleshy premonition no one wants to acknowledge, prematurely middle-aged even by the yardstick of a place where middle age can strike in one's twenties. So for sixteen years, Connie hovers along, at home, at school, a background noise, someone glimpsed only from corners of eyes, never interesting enough to hate and not even ugly enough to be noticed. And still, Jolo, that summer, chooses her.

Summers where they live. A dull pressure for three long months, a season that squats, the dirt itself on the verge of busting, everything full, until it feels like you, too (especially at fourteen, fifteen, at sixteen), are going to bust. Full. Connie grows up among plants more than people, they all do, and how they strain, strain to bust open, into berry, nut, seedpod, corn ear, like they're beings that run sap, not blood. And that summer, nearly every other night, Jolo covers eight miles on a single-speed banana-seat bike, most of the eight down off the mountain in the dark and all of the miles dark back up, Jolo moving. The bicycle lit by a single reflector and Jolo too big for the frame, him crunched high over the metal, moving, a praying mantis on miniature wheels. He is living that summer with his grandparents, old-timey types who don't own a phone, but a booth stands near enough their house, out on that county road, that Jolo can hear it from his bedroom window. Connie lets it ring and ring and ring, while Jolo jogs out to the booth and lifts the receiver. And then they have nothing to say.

Yes, for the first two months, they communicate only by hand.

Connie waits along the river on a fraying afghan. Connie crouched there in that river odor, the odor of things dead and things going to be born, and the great organ of insect, mounting, mounting, until she hears Jolo's bike bending the brush. He reaches her, and they already know there is nothing to say, so he just drops down, and they move together. They're moving. The night fishermen across the water, mumbly drunk, to be avoided, and the single night train, baying its lonesomeness, and the corn pollen a green sensation in the back of their throats, not quite smell, not quite taste. They are moving. Jolo's stomach, his back, glow glossy even in the dark, maybe more so in the dark, and he takes Connie's hand, and he says, "Here. Put your fingers on it."

No, they say very little for the first two months, June, July, so for a long time Connie knows only the county's version of the fire eleven years ago. A scare-parable parents tell children who mess with matches. So Jolo's family wiggles through Connie's dreams long before she remembers seeing them for real, a gallery of flaming fragments, images half imagined and half heard. She sees the gooey soles of Jolo's father's melting boots, him sprawled unconscious on the couch. Jolo's mother plummeting out a window on one side of the house, his aunt Ruby Nickelson charging into the opposite side to rescue her own son, Bony (now known by his pulpit name, Little Pastor Dan). Jolo's abandoned baby brother, a black thing, curled in a burned-up bed. And once in a great while, she'll picture Jolo boy himself— this one blurry, cartoonish, hard to imagine, until that summer Jolo chooses her—yes, little Jolo, four years old, stumbling out of a wall of fire, all on his own. That-Vix-boy-got-burned-up-so-bad-in-that-house-fire-up-Webb-Mountain is what the county calls Jolo, so by the time Connie is five or six, just the words "Webb Mountain" come dragging that chain: passed-out father, broken mother, saviored cousin, dead baby, charred Jolo.

But Jolo, when he starts talking, later, in August, when after their moving, Jolo will stay awhile, Jolo tells Connie that the fire was not the first time. He tells her that the first time he was even tinier, an infant in his playpen, and a stray cat got into his room. The cat snuck under his covers and started to draw his breath out his mouth, nearly suffocated him dead before his father found them and beat the cat bloody with a metal trash can. "Your mother told you?" Connie asks. "No. No," Jolo says, "I remember." And just a few years after the fire, up in New Jersey, a bunch of them were in a bad wreck that killed the one cousin who got thrown out of the car and ruined Jolo's mother's teeth, Jolo tells her, saying he can't remember that time, was knocked too hard in the head. And there have been times since, Jolo says. He won't say what.

Gradually he tells her it's not that something is trying to kill him, but that he'd just never been full-born. Says a part of him was left on some earlier other side and keeps trying to pull him back with it. Says church does nothing for him because it's the past, not the future, that gives him the tug. And each time he beats it, he comes at the spirit in another way. And although Jolo's cousin, Bony, has become a child evangelist, Jolo tells her, no. God doesn't go to revivals. Says, no. God don't go to no revivals.

God.

When Connie creeps into the barely double bed she shares with her ten-year-old sister, she does not sleep. She reaches back and cups every spent minute in her hands. The grit of the silt between her legs and the sheets, the grit in her pants, she reaches back and unbraids every minute into separate strands—touch, taste, smell, sound—and she fondles them, a second time, a third, a fourth, and even though she's alone, there is little diminishment, he, they, are that strong, that big (Connie is learning).

But her little sister starts to snore. Not loud, but enough to put a smear on things. Connie raises onto an elbow and studies her, biscuit-colored, bland and saggy, her mouth leaking onto her pillow. Then the hall floor creaks, and Connie listens to her mother shuffling to the toilet, one arm, Connie knows, braced against a wall. And the old hate wakes up inside Connie, despite that she swallows on it, hard, Connie can't help but hate her sister—her mother, her father, herself—hate her sister for her limp hair, her sinus infections, for the way she fades back and watches. Fades. Nearly every other night when Connie wedges herself out the first-story window, her parents sit stupored by some television show, suspecting nothing. Their oldest daughter, as far as they're concerned, as sexual as a potato. Now her mother shuts the bathroom door behind her as if there's somebody to watch. Connie hears water hit water.

She looks again at her sister, apologizes in her mind and tries to mean it. She touches the back of her hand to her sister's forehead, like checking for a fever, but her sister's skin feels cooler than the air. Connie rolls away. She sticks her fingers in her ears and tries again. She mouths it, tongues it, Jolo, Jolo boy, and what it calls up in her, slip-

peried together with the silt and the muck. The weed
smells, the bed of the river. Old, old mud.

Because Connie starts to remember. All spun in on herself, curling tighter and tighter, she decides she remembers.
By July, she is wondering, then she starts to remember,
and, at last, in August, after Jolo tells her about the wreck
and the cat and God, she believes. That Jolo found her very
early on.

She remembers being four years old and riding rough in
the front seat, the vents throwing odor from a mouse nest
burnt up in the truck motor some time before. The pickup
pulls a dirt road not much better than a jeep track, lunging
at it the way an animal would. Her father, still healthy
then, still of a piece, swings her out of the cab and carries
her over the mud, and Connie watches him try to walk the
rut sides in his good shoes. Then she can see a small half-
built house in a bulldozed pit, part of this house mud-
splattered vinyl siding, part naked insulation, its yard a
yellow muck. Her father sets her down and tells her to stay
outside. Planks have been thrown over the yard muck, and
her father wobbles across them to the porch where he
scrapes mud off his shoes with a stick that he carries.

At the rear of the house, Connie finds a peculiar man
kneeling at a window on a heap of sodden carpet rolls.
And suddenly, this peculiar man, retarded somehow, or
crippled up, a man's head on a child's body, slides off the
carpets. He snatches her under her arms and hoists her to
the sill.

At first the shock makes her squeal. But then her wonder
takes her. She cups her hands around her eyes to dampen
her reflection and see inside. Two coffins, both closed, one
papa-sized, one baby. And, then, Connie can see (although
she's not at all sure, eleven years later, in June, she becomes
more sure in July, and by August, she stands convinced,

even though in June, into July, she understands that he could not have been at that house, would have been at the burn center in Baltimore), Connie sees, legs dangling from his mother's lap, a little boy about her own size.

He wears nothing but a pair of shorts, despite the cold, and he is naked in other ways, strange ways, as well. Naked where his eyebrows should be, his chest naked of its nipples, his head ragged bald across its crown where hair sprouts struggle like weeds in a rock face. But what stuns Connie hardest lies between his ribs and his shorts, because this part of his body glistens a liquid glass. This part looks to her (now, as she remembers, having since seen such storms) like the aftermath of an ice storm, every limb on every ridge transfigured to a rumpled prism. The one ear has melted to a twist. A little bud unopened.

*   *   *

Her father doesn't remember the visit at all. Yes, Connie brings it up the summer she's fifteen, she cannot resist, even though she believes it is dangerous, thinking surely that even if they don't notice the sneaking out, her parents can't help but feel the change off her. Despite the risk, Connie brings it up to him one evening, there in the open door of the metal utility shed where her father bides his time like a dog in a pen. But he does not remember. Not the road, not the mud, not the burned-up boy. Her father only remembers the jars.

"Remember the jars?" he says. "For months after that fire, was a mayonnaise jar on every store counter in this end of the county. Had a picture of the boy taped on front, taken before he got all fried up. They say the father started it, you know, passed out drunk smoking a cigarette. I went to school with the old boy, never was much count. Anyway, they had spaghetti dinners, rummage sales, ramp feeds, fifty-fifty raffles, I don't even know what all."

He pauses to spit in his styrofoam cup, and Connie can see the photo in her head. A K-Mart studio photo of little Jolo, pinkly skinned, and under that, a caption explaining the fire, the hospital bills, no insurance. Jolo becomes a community project, the Christian thing to do, but after about a year, her father says, Jolo's mother publishes a Notice of Appreciation in the county's weekly paper and they all disappear into New Jersey.

"So you can imagine," her father goes on, "when they show back up here five years later with the boy looking like a glazed doughnut. All that praying and fundraising for nearly nothing. Send him to Baltimore on the county nickel and end up with . . . what? Some cut-rate job for hicks." Her father falls silent, shifts his bulk in his lawn-chair. When he heaves himself out for the evening, Connie knows it will hang all night with his print. "Yeah, some cut-rate job for hicks," he says, and he changes the subject to the heat.

But this doesn't matter. Connie can tell it herself from there. Because the first day of fifth grade, Jolo shows up on Connie's bus run, Connie recovering that day now, six years later, over and over in those nights she doesn't sleep, Connie understanding, gradually, how it all falls together. Five years after they disappear into New Jersey, Jolo's mother returns without the second husband and moves herself, Jolo, and his sister, Pelia, into a bankrupted bait shop on the hill above Connie's house—*Connie's* house. Of course, Connie doesn't know they're back as she climbs onto Bus 14 in her first-day-of-school clothes, already, at ten years old, both excruciatingly self-conscious and completely unnoticed, but five minutes later, the bus startles everyone by pulling over at the abandoned store. Jolo's mother has tried to disguise the place with curtains in the display windows and fake poinsettias on the bait coolers out front, although they never do get rid of the RC sign; they just bust out the store name with rocks and live under the RC logo alone. But all this Connie will notice later, because that first day of fifth grade, the only thing she and everyone else notice are the two new kids, and after registering that there are two, no one gives a second look to the girl.

He swings up into that bus shameless and shockful (Jolo boy). Not only does he go hatless over the skull, the curdled ear, a snail shell buttoned, but for his first day at his new school, Jolo wears one of those football jerseys made of wide loose mesh. Through the mesh they glimpse tiny teases of waxy skin. The horror and the glory in little lacquered dots. They half spy the scarlet furrows over his chest, the nipples or not? and Bus 14 falls quiet as a graveyard. Jolo drops easy into an empty seat as if he's the only person there.

From that day on, to be within eyeshot of Jolo for all the kids is a constant deliberate looking-away, a knowing better than to stare—both because of how they are raised and because of the looks Jolo gives back—but unable to resist, as though Jolo's skin has been injected with tiny magnets that suck eyes. And it's like this for Connie, too, she is no different, but only Bobby Wheazel, who is very special ed, forgets to know better and, day in and day out, gets his eyes full, until that summer Jolo chooses her. And in the meantime, the grown-ups muttering, the botched plastic surgery, confirmation of their suspicion of the overeducated and uppity, all that fundraising and praying for . . . just look at this. But it is really no big surprise. They are brought up to expect disappointment. What they can't know, Connie neither, at that time, is that it's not the doctor's fault at all. What they can't know is that Jolo's mother simply didn't keep up with the rehab. And now, this summer, Connie learns not only that his mother didn't keep up, but that Jolo sees this as a gift.

"We used to call him Bony, but now he goes by his pulpit name, Dan," Jolo says once afterwards while Connie lies on the dirty afghan, filled so rich inside for Jolo she feels her chest split open and butter spill out. Jolo does not touch her. He sits with his back against a sycamore, knees drawn to his chest, his thighs covering the places where the nipples should be. He does not touch her, but Connie can feel the current off him anyway. "Mom would keep him Saturdays while Aunt Ruby cooked at the VFW, and Ruby'd just leave him down to our place all night so she wouldn't have to wake him."

The river funk carries a memory kind of smell, the deep to it, and Jolo stirs round and round in the dirt with a branch. Aunt Ruby Nickelson and Bony moved away after the fire even faster than Jolo's family did, but even so . . . Bony still sticks to Jolo, a crusted rash. A rash that has flared up pitiless on him since that Wednesday night in early June when his grandparents came back from the Church of the Brethren where they'd heard the news that Bony, now called Dan, was expected in August on the revival circuit. Little Pastor Dan, regionally renowned for his come-to-Jesus voice, an altar call they say, like butterflies in his throat. A child evangelist delivered from a house fire at the age of three without a scar, by the grace of God delivered. Jolo gouges at the dirt with his stick. And it's coming to him now, more pressing every day, how it's time to do what he's meant to do.

"So Ruby was up the road at her place when the fire broke out, but she beat the fire trucks to it. Claims she just knew. It was Al Chance saved Pelia off the porch roof, he was Fire Chief back then. Then Mom, she jumped out the window and left little Charlie behind. She got heavy into the religion afterwards, the guilt and all. Before, we'd just been Church of the Brethern, but then she turned Assembly, and finally Holy Temple of Praise. That's another reason I moved in with Grandma and them. Too much church at Mom's."

"Like what? What kind of stuff do they do?" Connie has sat up with the listening. She's been raised tepid Methodist in a place where most churches like their spirits live. Her own religion she sees a neutered gray in the midst of all these mysteries, tangled and hot, and she has always sensed it, steaming off of Jolo, even though Jolo insists his faith is of a different kind.

Jolo just grunts.

"Oh. You know. That holy roller shit." His stick snaps off in the ground.

The insect song heartbeats out of the weeds, surge and recede, surge and recede. Jolo's ears follow it, pattern it, memory it . . . The snak-snak of the drumkit, an underswell of bass guitar, the great "UHH"s the preacher'd insuck after every phrase, and then they'd be moving. They'd be up and moving. They preached the endtimes every Sunday, Social Security numbers, they said, the Mark of the Beast, and they held their hands over their heads when they prayed like they were asking a question, but with the palms facing down like the answer didn't matter. Jolo waits for the Holy Spirit. He grinds his teeth and tries. And pretty soon, all the others are moving, they're up and moving, leaving only Jolo and the elderly disabled behind. Jolo chill and rigid as a nickel, he sees his heart as a nickel, he does, and all the God in the place swirls Jolo right by.

It's his mother makes him continue to go. His mother, born and born and born again, and you know the state of her spirit by the clothes that she wears, those dull flappy dresses when she walks with the Lord. Then she'll backslide into her favorite black jeans, them fitting her like a snakeskin, and the pointy high-heeled boots, and her little belly, only fat part on her—she is made long and dark and flat—paunching out over her waistband. Like a blacksnake swallowed a robin's egg, Jolo is thinking. And sometimes she stays backslid for months, once a whole year, and that is better, he knows, that is better. But in the meantime, when she's saved, she dresses him up and drags him to church. His skinny butt numbed on metal chairs, pine pews, molded plastic. In New Jersey, in West Virginia, once at a big revival in Ashland, Kentucky, the others moving and Jolo left behind. Then, one day in Sunday School, they learn about Daniel.

Those years in New Jersey, before he understood, how he kept himself covered. Long-sleeved cowboy shirts, snapped snug at the wrists, even in summer, and T-shirts under those, just to be safe, and a toboggan pulled low over his scalp, the ear. One afternoon in the New Jersey elementary school, he is cornered in the bathroom. They pin him on the floor and strip off the cowboy shirt, part of the T, Jolo's raw skull scraping the concrete as he strikes at them with his teeth. They throw the cap in a urinal. They start to rip down his pants. A teacher storms in and calls them off, but Jolo sees: Even the teacher is more curious than concerned, and this strikes Jolo. This strikes him. Jolo pulls himself up against a stainless steel stall and zips his pants. He stumbles back two steps and stares at his naked torso, warpled in the reflection there.

The Sunday they learn about Daniel, he steals the Bible comic book and studies the pictures at home in his room, the fiery furnace, the three moving, cubits and cornets, kings nibbling grass. And Jolo starts to understand. His own body, in Baltimore, all bound in white, he begins to remember, bound up in his garments, garments, he calls them, a Bible word, and Jolo starts to see. It is the past, not the future, that gives him the tug. He takes to locking himself in his bedroom, a chair jammed under the knob, and he unsnaps the shirt and reads his skin. Its brightness, how it moves on him, its light, how it gleams. He sees it lustered in perfection, a thing not of the here and now, and he starts to remember the night he walked through.

Chosen. Extraordinary. What makes him himself.

By the time he is twelve, thirteen, back in West Virginia, he knows. He bathes, pulls the plug from the drain, stands up to dry. His trunk a sea of glass, him mirroring the mirror.

"But God don't go to church," he tells Connie. "And He sure as hell don't go to no revivals."

Connie nods, and sidles a little closer to him, but Jolo doesn't notice. He swallows. "I walked through fire," he says. "Bony was carried out, and that was different."

"That was different," he says.

That summer's fires begin in late July. They are set in buildings always empty somehow: second homes, a video store closed for the night, a barn on a bankrupt farm. Connie hears about them, everybody does, but she gives them little thought—she has plenty else to think on—until the deputy sheriff in the grocery store lot. Around that time, Jolo starts coming less often, but speaks to her more. Touches her afterwards in places that aren't private, so that even Connie, who has expected all summer to be abandoned at any moment, can tell he's not leaving her yet.

But she has to make do, more and more often, with the meeting place itself. She finds herself back along the river in the days, because to place herself there, even in full light, is to conjure an imprint of the nights, and now she craves them all the time. The insect voice, collapsed thin and lacey in the sun, but the moisture, the blood temperature, amplified, oozing. The air exactly the same wetness, the same heat, inside her lungs and out, the air itself is lungy, so Connie can't track her own breathing, again, she is continuous, and she's moving. She's moving past the beer and bait trash, the stubbed-out little fires. Moving past the dirty foam boiled up in the river's elbows, and she feels for it, feels pity for the river, a river full of chicken shit and rain. She feels deep and feels for everything these days, all her feeling parts poised out on the edges of her skin, bared, and Connie, who has never before been touched by a boy, a man, now believes that it *is* the keloid that makes her feel, that carries with it the tight wet charge. And she's moving, wallowing in the shape of what's left over from the nights . . . but she's also dodging poison and itchweed, the small and evil plants, and always, the Jolo-conjuring diluted a little by her watching for snakes. Because that is what it is to move there in the summer. Always, a periphery of snakes.

In August, the week Little Pastor Dan arrives, there are two more fires, and Connie grows more certain. One evening on the way to the Dairy Queen, her family passes the revival. The tent is set up where you can't see it from the road—better to build the suspense—but they read the signs—"Teenage Evangelist" "Ghost-Filled Revival"—and gawk at the pasture full of parked automobiles. Connie's mother mentions she'd like to hear those butterflies, and Connie tells her fine, but Connie's not going to no revival. Yet, six straight days that week, Jolo doesn't come to her.

She pauses now, there on the riverbank, late morning, the light wet and down low. She squats, and her thighs flatten out like some great underwings. Last night she listened to the sirens, less than an hour after she gave up waiting

and crawled back into bed, and by ten o'clock that morning, she'd heard that it had been another weekend home,
this one up on Shake Mountain. And she has called the
phone booth, again and again, the ringer a mechanical locust in her ear, but nobody has answered. Still, Connie
doesn't worry. It was after the second fire she'd been ques-
tioned by the cop, and at that time, the idea of Jolo as ar-
sonist had scared her. It had. But she feels different about it
since then.

She feels irradiated by it since then.

Because this is what it is to grow up between long tun-
nelly ridges, never considered one who'd get out, never
grouped with that handful who might amount to something, absolutely nothing about you to be noticed, remembered. Not even deserving the favoritism granted the lowli-
est boys. To see beyond high school only pregnancy or
marriage, whichever comes first, a honeymoon to Smoke
Hole Caverns, the hope that your children don't hurt you
too bad. But at the same time, to be susceptible, raised to
obedience and easy belief. Until you piece it all together
and finally know that you have been chosen by that body
who walked through fire. And you feel big for the first time
in your life.

Because Jolo did tell it, eventually, gradually, he told it,
not as a story, not in lines, he told it in circles, concentric
circles, each circle widening, filling, taking on flesh, and
Connie absorbs it like that, receiving it in a sedimentation,
the mesh thickening, livening, assuming texture and depth.
And by the time he's told maybe eight, ten circles, Connie
has it in her head like this: Jolo saying,

"It was Aunt Ruby coming in there woke me at all. Not
the smoke or the heat, I would of slept dead through those.
But when Bony stayed over, he slept in the bed with Charlie and me, and I woke to the bounce in the springs when

she snatched Bony up. Then I was coughing. Terrible coughing, jerking my head around so I couldn't hardly see, the coughing all mixed up with the stink of Bony's piss in the covers, and Charlie, he wasn't making a sound. Not a sound. Him over there on the far side the bed where we slept, him against the wall so he wouldn't tumble out. No, I didn't even think to check on Charlie. I remember sitting up and sliding onto the floor, and I remember the heat on the flat of my feet. Then I don't remember for a while.

"Next thing I know, I'm at the top of the stairs, and I can see, even through all the smoke and flame, I can see Aunt Ruby barreling away towards the front door—she's a big woman in a big green coat, easy to see even through all that—and Bony slung over her shoulder with his mouth squawled open. They're already a good ways gone. Ruby with her back to me.

"So I stand there at the top of those stairs, coughing, smoke-tears rolling down my face, and, buddy, what a noise. Everything ripping and crashing, stuff blowing up. Then, it shuts up. Just like that. Like a hand cupping down over it, pinching it out.

"The noise shut up, and I couldn't hear nothing but my own blood rushing through me. Yeah, like I was a wee little gnat swimming my own blood, and it goes like this: WHOOOOM. WHOOOOM. WHOOOOM. WHOOOOM. Then I look over my shoulder down the hall and see flames jabbing out from under every last door. And then I know. It's coming for me.

"Yeah, then I feel it. I feel myself being pulled backwards, sucked backwards, like that. Yeah, it's put a drag on me, and I glide backwards a little, and I feel my insides start to cave like a sand washing down, and I know I'm going.

"I was scooting back cross the floor, and I had my hands flung out like maybe I could stop myself, but I couldn't touch anything, the walls had drawn away, and my bare feet were picking up splinters and coals . . . when something put the brakes on me. Something reached down and handled me. And it snapped me to a stop and it stiffened my guts, and then, lo and behold, I'm moving ahead.

"Then I'm moving. I know exactly where to put my feet on those burning stairs, and once I reach the bottom, I keep knowing. Not only do I know where to find the doors in the smoke, I know where the walls are down, I'm moving. I pass through. Not only do I know where the walls are down, I know where the flames are thinnest, I can move through. I'm not scared, and I watch, and it's a beautiful thing. How it burns the different colors when it catches different things, colors you ain't never seen before, colors ain't even been thought up. I watch how it takes its time on some things, like it's loving them up, and how it hurries on the others. The paneling and curtains just zipping along, and the wallpaper running backwards to nothing the way a hornet's nest will when you torch it. And Daddy's deerheads, them smoldering, those go slow, and I pass the phone melting off the hook, and the linoleum, melting, me tracking in it like mud, and then that old trunk we had down there, come from up at Grandmommy's place, I see its lid fry open and little things flee out. I did.

"And I'm moving. I'm moving. And I don't feel or hear a single thing but blood ripping through my body and veins until I pass through the front of that house and hit the coldest air there ever was. And one of them jumped me and rolled me on the ground, and then all of it, the roaring and crashing and screams, come back over me like a thunderstorm."

Then Jolo stops. His voice drops down. It's just louder than a whisper, raspy. Prayerful. Connie leans closer, prickled in her skin.

"And you know that Bible story?"

Connie looks at him, expectant. He gazes at the dark and goes on.

"The ShadrachMeshachAbednego fire?"

Connie nods.

Jolo says, "The ones watching the furnace door, they said: 'And the fourth one, he looks like an angel.'"

Jolo turns to Connie. She's huddled on the quilt, clutching her knees, and she can feel it, currenting off him, she can. She feels her own spirit harden, lengthen, with what currents off of Jolo, now them believing together, and she starts to understand herself for the first time in her life. Jolo reaches for her hand. He lays it on his stomach. The graft tissue is a perfect surface, skin that doesn't even sweat.

"See?" Jolo says. "Purified it, He did. Breath of God."

Jolo answers the pay phone the last day of the revival. Later that afternoon, after Connie sets the table for supper, she kneels in the wind off the lint-caked box fan. Her hair streams back, and she feels the strain under her skin, so full it is, and Connie gasps a little.

She catches herself. Glances sideways, wonders if her mother heard her. But her mother keeps flouring slices of yellow squash, sliding them into hot oil. Beyond her mother, her sister, on her stomach in the living room, and Connie can tell her apart from the cement-colored carpet only by the TV glint off her glasses, her sister fading. Fading. As though she has been drained off into the television, as though that is the way the wires work. Her mother keeps rocking, back and forth, counter to stove, dripping from her arms, her throat, flesh the color of an unbaked crust. Connie turns away and coos into the fan. Her voice returns as the insect chirr. She quivers. She lifts up on her haunches in the breeze off the fan, she unfolds her arms, and the wind catches the perspiration under them and chills her, pimples her, and Connie knows how she is two of a kind.

As soon as her sister starts to snore, Connie's out the first-story window, across the yard, and over the railroad embankment. Then she's moving through the river bottom. She's moving among the plants, them pumping under their barks, their peels, and the bugs orchestrating, piles upon piles, the nearest layer always hushing as soon as she gets close, the sound always one film beyond her. She reaches the tiny clearing their bodies have rubbed in the weeds, and she drops heavy over the bank to pull the afghan out of the little cave the eroded roots make there.

She knows he will be late, but by this time, she can induce it almost completely without him. She is that strong. She lies on the afghan, and she can feel in her hand the graft scars left on his thighs, his behind, the smoothness runneled. And she listens to a single nearby cricket, banjo pick, a live pick, pulled across Jolo's keloid-rippled chest. She shuts her eyes, and the sights she spells up lightning between that first fire and these recent ones. She enters Jolo and fills him behind his skin, and they move. They know where to pass, the fire shucking off their bodies, them moving, extraordinary. From inside Jolo's eyeballs she watches as they pass through the second homes, the carpet ablaze in ten thousand tiny loops, knick-knacks shattering off shelves, ammunition catching in gun cabinets and the rifles firing holes through the roof. Through the video store, reels of tape whipping about like nests of evaporating serpents. She watches as they move through the old barn, flushed swallows and mud daubers swarming their head, silos like Roman candles, flames racing down mangers like fuses lit. And she keeps going, she moves through each fire until the one he's told her he'll set tonight. A little fire, just a practice fire. It's an old railroad shed about a mile and a half away, a place where they used to store equipment, not much bigger than a one-car garage, and it shouldn't take long. Then Connie heaves herself out of Jolo's body and slingshots eleven years into the distance, and she lights down in a hickory tree outside that burning house on Webb Mountain, and she watches Jolo boy, four years old, surface from that first fire, seething all over with flames, but not destroyed, no, spectaculared, Jolo crackled glorious all over, and Connie pops her eyes open in awe.

Connie waits a very long time. She waits so long she finally falls asleep a little, and when she wakes up, she's chilled despite the season. She clambers back over the bank to hide the afghan and head for home, but she's only a little disappointed. She stays hopeful for tomorrow.

She's almost to the tracks when she smells gasoline. It comes to her bright against the vegetation smells. She understands immediately and stops. Then Jolo steps out of the weeds and fills the smell, and although at first Connie can only see him as a blacker place against the blackish brush, when she moves right up on him, she sees the sweaty T-shirt is not scorched or singed and she believes it has worked again. She puts her body against him. He doesn't touch her back, but that's not unusual. Connie can hear his heart going in him, she listens.

Jolo grabs the fat part of her arm, and he is not gentle. He jerks her along the trail towards the tracks. They scrabble through the rockfill up the embankment, Connie slipping in the loose gravel and banging her knee, and then Jolo yanks her down so they're sitting side by side on the rail. Connie, her knee throbbing, her weight jabbed by the narrow rail, Connie still yearns at Jolo. Although it's too dark to see much, she squints down at Jolo's hands and arms to view their savioring, a sight she's never seen so fresh. And untouched they are, not a hair crisped. But then she notices the hands are trembling, and she looks him in the face. When Jolo finally speaks, he does so through clenched teeth.

"*You* know why I set them," he says.

"To make a fire big enough to walk through," she answers. She waits. They are not touching. "What's the matter?" she says.

He wipes his mouth in the bottom of the filthy shirt and turns away.

"What's the matter?" she says again. They are not touching. The railroad holds the day's heat, heavy in its ties, and now it fumes up, filling them from the bottom, a weight to it Connie feels settle in her jaws.

"I haven't yet," he answers.

"What do you mean?" Connie asks.

"I haven't walked through yet."

Connie's lungs begin to go faster, but lighter. Like little moths dissolving in her chest. After a while, she reaches her insides toward Jolo, but she gets nothing back. Her mind suddenly finds itself with no place to go. She drifts in a dark that has nothing to do with the river bottom at night, the sound of this dark like a shell to her ear, and she feels in her heart a tiny draining backwards. Then she understands, in a way without words, that she straddles a gully, the gully widening, and one side of her stays with the boy who walked through. But her other side senses, in the middle distance, with an unfocused but gut-deep panic . . . that side backpedaling, but nonetheless sensing, Jolo's terrible ordinariness.

She braces her hands behind her on the rail and starts to struggle to her feet, not because she plans to leave, but because she might get her bearings there. Jolo snatches her back by her belt loop.

"Don't worry," he says. "I figured out what's wrong."

So Connie settles back down. On either side of her hips, she grips the rail still warm from the hours-gone sun. She repeats in her head what Jolo's said, twice. Places one warm hand on her rapid chest, coaxes her lungs to slow themselves. Connie waits. She screws up her will and tries. And, then, gradually, the roar in her ears diminishes, and she hears what she'd stopped listening to: the great organ of insect. Its surge and recede, the sobbing mesh, layers of ankles and throats and wings, it washes back, an extension of Connie, the noise shirring the rind of her head, the kernel of her chest, until her breath beats the same meter as the creatures and trees. And rushing over her comes the age in Jolo, like the age in Connie. But with Connie, the age is in the body, and with Jolo, it's deeper someplace.

Then finally she's moving. She is moving, towards that soul who walked through, and she understands, and she starts to say. Say *Jolo,* she tells herself. *Jolo.* Softly at first, she tells herself, *Jolo,* then loud as the pitch of the insect throb, say *Jolo, Jolo boy,* and finally with conviction, she is saying, *Jolo,* say *Jolo,* and you'll know, *Jolo,* she tells herself, *say it,* and Jolo says,

"With the two of us, it'll work."

WAPPATOMAKA

=

Go rinse that rocker, my father tells me, and he speaks for the first time all day from a place I cannot see, the dark covering quick now. Though it is November, it is unseasonable warm, and I can smell the stuff begin to rot. His old rabbit dog Buster is coiled on himself in the rocker seat under the porch eaves. When the water came five days ago, Buster holed up in the house with my father while the rest of us got out. He swam in the back door when we first opened it and didn't shake off until he climbed the highest bed in the second story. I cannot see to wash, and all the scrubwater we have left is a silty few inches in the bottom of an ice cream tub, but I roust Buster and slosh at the chair just to give my father some peace. The rocker was where my grandfather sat on the days he would come downstairs. Buster and my father waited it out until the river crested, sopped the rugs on the upper floor, and dropped. The collie dog ran off and never came back. We paddled out, my mother and me and the little boys, the rain let up then and the moon all bared.

I feed Bus after I rinse the chair, give him the crust at the bottom of a big casserole someone sent over and a can of pork and beans, label soaked away. They say on WXLD throw out even your canned goods, store-bought or not. On the hill, the Kesslers had kept their radio going and I know it was not good luck to listen. *Jay Wence, get in touch with your parents, Mrs. Esta Mae Teeter wants to let her family know she is safe, anyone knowing the whereabouts of Randy or Markle Fox, call 547-6818.* It went on and on. I stand at the edge of the backyard in the muck and holler up the mountain for the other dog because this is her suppertime and it has been five days. But she stays wherever she is.

We paddled in that moon toward the hill, us picking through the debris in the backwater, then I was jabbing ground and I looped the canoe line around the Kesslers' gate. My mother carried my biggest brother and I waded the other, his ankles buckled around my waist and him whimpering hot in my hair. We waited it out in the Kesslers' garage with the door drawn open, listened to it all roll down and hit. And it was not just trees and then not just trailers crashing against the bridge across Route 50, finally it was houses, too. And the sycamores popping like rifles. In a rusty glider in the corner of the garage, my mother, creaking, her face crumpled into her scarf. By kerosene lamp Mrs. Kessler cooked the boys hot dogs on her grill. The radio ranted the lost.

That collie dog ain't coming back, my father tells me. I settle two chairs down from him in one of my great-grandmother's Windsor dining room chairs, grit on the arms. I put my hands in my jacket pockets, not thinking, scare myself and jerk them free. I've forgotten what I'm carrying and I've never been much on the dark. Our house is inside out still, just about all we own laid out in the yard so the fire company could come today. They sprayed the worst of the mud off the floors, the walls. Had to spray out every square foot even though we haven't had the whole place opened up in my lifetime. Room after room in the back jumpled up with mildew-scummed furniture and odds and ends needing fixed. Half-wild cats traveling in and out the broken windows and live things in the chimneys. Clive McDermott driving the fire truck said we were lucky, said nearly forty people drowned, worst flood in the history of the South Branch. Said they'd be looking for bodies soon as it unmuddied. We played hide-and-seek in those back rooms when my cousins still lived around here, and once they latched me in a wardrobe and left me behind. I balled my eyes so shut I went white in my head. My grandfather died in a bloody way up there when I was five. Cattle in tops of trees, Clive said, people from Mouth of Seneca drifting six miles on a piece of silo, found dead still clutching the tile. Families up in the Petersburg gap trying to burn their houses before the water hit in hopes of collecting fire insurance. Nobody had been able to afford flood.

Bus walks over to get his ears rubbed, the smell off him all rank and greazy. I walked the Big Bottom with him this afternoon, looking for the body of the collie dog.

They come mostly from the church to help us clean up, what family we have left moved away from here to find work. My father shuts himself in the pickup before they come. He sits there under the walnut tree all day. You can see his head a knob over the back of the seat, shoulders tucked up around his ears. He knows it's to no purpose, the washing, the fixing. A wine glass had floated out the corner cupboard and set itself nice on the dining room table for us when we first walked back in. Half full, soil slicked across the bottom and settled in the stem. You will always remember that, my mother told me. I had never seen a goblet leave that cupboard. My mother and the boys sleep at the preacher's house where I know she sends those puny prayers at night, them filtering out the window cracks with no more force than the dust on the sills. She walks the ruined road at first light to get out here and clean. But my father won't leave the house, so I stay with him. No power, no running water. Every evening in his grandmama's chairs on the porch, in the smell of the dead things spoiling.

I walked the Big Bottom with Buster today. Flattest place I've seen, broadest, and to be there of a winter, mountains opened wide, dizzying it is. An honest kind of scared. It is gutted now. Acres and acres of my father's land washed downstream, acres thrown full of river rock. Bus snuffled the towers of drift, unburied a whole ham from the Moorefield Foodland, that eighteen miles upriver. He found it in a snag of equipment I knew we still owed on, hung up in some maples that didn't go out. Then Buster spooked. Shied forty yards away from a trench near the bank of the river, wheeled, then paced an edge I could not see.

You will always remember that, my mother told me, the wine glass. Like someone set the table. There was no real warning. My father set his alarm for 2:00 to check the stove and it was ankle-deep downstairs by then. With the boys too small to be of any use, the three of us carried stuff upstairs by candle, my father making us take the guns first and then the photo albums got spoiled, river rippling up my pants-legs and the candlelight lapping on top that muddy water. I tell you, I've never been much on the dark. Things coasting by, things thumping, the stray rug wrapping round my leg. The boys huddled with Buster on my mother's bed, that great black headboard looming behind, the youngest lowing steady. Lowing. The year before my grandfather died he slept in a different room every night.

I'd lie listening to him shuffle crosst the floors. We carried up until it was over our waists, then me and the rest paddled out. I turned around in that booming moon to see if anything was coming behind.

Buster shied and paced an edge I could not see, moaning and jogging his weight on his bowlegs. They say the river dammed itself up behind the railroad trestle on the far side of the Trough, and when the pressure finally blew it out, it came a wall of water. We were six miles below. The current furrowed the Bottom as deep as my knees, tunneled and cratered it. I stumbled in to where Bus had spooked. We would stand here, my father and me, when I was very small, and over the mountains, live-gray in February like they are, pussy-willow, he would stroke his hand and name them to me. Those mountains went after my grandfather did. I stumbled in to where Bus had run. At the bottom of the furrow a face lay buried up to its eyesockets. I dropped down, Bus pacing and worrying. I scrabbled at it and pulled it free, saw his jaw was lost, saw how the mud had worked webs in the skull dome.

Mrs. Kessler sang Bible School songs with the boys, her in her wool skirt and waders, *Jesus loves the little children, all the children of the world.* And a half mile away the weight of the water on the tracks had set off the train crossing bell and it beat time for all the rest, the radio, the thunderstrokes against the bridge, the *Jesus loves* and the creaking. My mother, a ripple of mud in a long overcoat, knuckling the sides of that rusty glider.

I let it be, the skull, lay it back tender and marked the spot with a piece of drift. Then I walked that skinned cornfield. I cradled the big bones under my arms, the pelvises, the thighs, carried the small ones, fingers and shards, careful in my pockets. They'd been flood-strewn a full mile down the bottom, jutting out the furrows, and sometimes

and told myself, "Do like Kenny is." So I jammed my
in, then my shoulders, and at first it didn't cave, but,
, I was tamped tight without a thing to see, and then I
myself screaming: "Groundhog! Groundhog!"
eah, they put hillbillies down those holes along with
ittle Hispanics, the blacks were mostly too big. And
now they used dogs first, but they lost too many?"
was Billy Blankenship talking, several years later.
may be right. From groundhog country we are, no
about that. Weasels and mushrats, beavers, snakes.
, rabbits, rats, there's holes just everwhere under our
our grandpap'll tell ya. Tunnel rats, they called em,
u may be right, more like a groundhog. A rat would
more leeway than Kenny and them ever did, but
dhogs I imagine, fat as they are, must get plugged in
tight, rippling along with the flubber flattening and
at the sides, and that's how it was. No, not rats."
y left out of here when I was six and he never came
ut I remember. Running those little bottoms, hunt-
bits in the multiflora rose, the blackberry vines,
ars in the backs of my hands. Me raggedy-lunged in
ember snap, dirt clods crumbling under my feet.
struggled to keep up with my big brother Kenny.
my half-brother, belonged to my mother before
married, and there was something wrong with the
learned, and he couldn't write well so he didn't
en. His letters from Vietnam, the three of them,
a puzzle or a secret code. Like you could hold
a mirror and they'd make a different sense. As a
would sit in closets muttering in tops of boots,
they tell on him. And he never did grow proper.
blamed it on Mom's clothes when she was carry-
Mommy finishing high school in a big plaid car
the belt cinched tight, "into April, into *May*,"

I'd reach down and close my hand on sponge and rot, the
bones stained the same yellow as the dead cornstalks there.
The flattest place I've ever stood, and the land, my father
would say. That's what will always be here for us. Me little
and the wind passing my corduroy pants and the only
thing we can count on. Raw now. Bloated deer caught up
in the wash, flint-colored like the trees and the ground, and
the long-ago people scattered to craziness. I gathered them.

I shiver on the porch in that unseasonable warm, my father buried in dark, just the bill of his cap and the thrust of
his nose, in the smell of the drowned things rotting. I've
got fingers in my pockets, I say to myself. And they're not
mine. But I am quiet. It is quiet on the porch. They used to
tell a lot of stories, back when my grandfather and my uncles were still around, stories that went way, way back, my
people coming on this piece of ground in 1773. And my
grandfather, when he was dressed and to himself and upright in his rocking chair, he used to tell a time he was fishing below the ford and spied in the silt there a musket ball
lying in a little whorl. And he traced, he said, the groove it
had made clear back into the bank where he saw it had
rolled out of the skull of a child clutching a bone comb
with its handle carved like a doll. He reburied her, my
grandfather said. But after he died, the others began to
wonder if it had been at all. They called it just a story, and
only my father was left to swear it, him a little boy then,
watching with a string of dying smallmouth bass slapping
feeble against his calf. There on the bank of what the little
girl would have called Wappatomaka.

In the day, from the house, they can barely see me, scudding across the Big Bottom like a piece of flood drift. Laziness, I imagine they think it is, her father's daughter, not
helping and so much to be done. Dawn to sunset washing
the earth away, I've carried bucket after bucket just off my

bedroom floor, raising the silt out the board cracks with a scrub brush and daubing it clean. And still, of a night, the odor of the riverbed all through the house, and I sleep with it soaking my head. Before I can dig the big hole, I have to have them all heaped together, and when I've stolen the hour or two, I hide them in the furrow under the dirt. I cover them light.

Wappatomaka. They say it means white ground.

It will have to be a deep hole, an all-night-long hole, else a spring flood will unsettle them again, or the new roads, someone's summer home after we're gone. Bus bellies down into a trench and waits for me, moon half washed away by now, and though the dark spooks me in a tight place and worries me worse in a big open like this one, I dig. The earth is damp and loose and cakes in the folds of my jeans. It moves easy. But on the way down, I hit another one, him all in one piece, and then what do you do? What do you do?

Buster does not bark. I catch him out the tail of my eye, my father, coasting cross the Big Bottom like a spirit in that long underwear he sleeps in, having woke, I understand all of a sudden, in the mazey black of the house, and found even me gone. Running towards me with his hands driving open and forward, like spades, and he bellows something I hear only as a question, the end of it lifting over my head, him sleepmurky and moonblind and in his boots. And I call out, stop, stop, but he is in the loose dirt already though he does not know it, until we both hear them brickle up under his feet.

The river is still up, hishing in the riffle. Wappatomaka. They say it means white ground. I drop my shovel because I am tired, heavy with this dirt in our veins.

DIRT

≡

This task demanded not only special skills, [...] cial type of temperament and courage. The [...] the most unnatural and stressful of tasks: [...] low, earthen tunnels for hundreds of yards [...] any moment. . . . In damp black holes du [...] most Americans found claustrophic panic [...] Cu Chi, by Tom Mangold and John Penyc [...]

Historically, young Appalachians have [...] the military and in combat situations. . . [...] or 85 for every 100,000 males in the sta[...] ita than any other state.—Caught Up In [...] lachian Vietnam Veterans, by John Hen[...]

I was seven when Kenny ser [...] doing, letter on wide-ruled [...] spots. Mommy slipped her [...] where she could be alone, [...] was crazy before he went [...] him so." Then I found me [...] door and up the railroad [...] dirt soft, with the smell [...] that groundhog hole feet [...]

Grandma told me. Mommy kept his baby pictures in a little cedar box Dad bought her at the honeymoon at Blackwater Falls, and Kenny looked wrong even then. Like a grub, a bleached-out thing blown over with fuzz. "All the time a-arching his back when you'd try to comfert eem," my grandma said. "Never would make up to no one much."

Billy Blankenship'd been over there, too, or I'd known even less than I did. It was Kenny and Billy and Roscoe McCracken went off this creek, left the War on Poverty for the One on Communism, but just Billy came back whole. They put what was left of Roscoe in the family cemetery where he washed out in an average sort of flood two springs later, buried like he was in a low place there, but nothing came back of Kenny. I'd visit Billy Blankenship, him laid up in his modular home with the heat forever cranked too high, gnawing on storebought popcorn. "They'd treat you like a king for five dollars a day," Billy would say, his bad knee propped on a cable spool and his beans boiling, whole place reeking of salt pork and earth. "Things you could see in Patphong, oh, you can't imagine, girls picking up baht pieces off Pepsi bottles with their you-know-what's. And then there was the fish bowls." He'd always stop right there to make me ask what were those because I was twelve by that time. "Go in, got all these girls sitting behind a one-way mirror with numbers pinned on their shirts—they're watching TV and can't see you, remember—and you pick one by her number. Like that. Fish bowls. Best year of my life, and I wasn't the only one."

"Billy! Don't be telling him that stuff." His wife, squeezing into her sewing factory uniform back in the bedroom. Billy did his tour in Thailand, flipped burgers in some mess hall in what you call U-bon Ratch-a-thani. Now he sat around eating storebought popcorn and spitting the hard pieces into a Hills Brothers can. Liked to take snapshots of stuff on the TV, organize them in photo albums. Stacked the albums up the sides of his chair and called them his Collection.

We snagged our war off an antenna Dad rigged in a tree, black-and-white screen and the fizzy reception. It snowed in our jungles. Holes, tunnels, dig your way to China, Alice fell through a tunnel, yeah, I liked that one. My brother dropped clear through the other side of the world. That summer after the letter we took to playing in the old Jenco store. Most of the kids stuck to the first and second floors, but me and Steve went down under. Moving like zombies in the pitch black, odor of cooped-up dirt, and the other kids thumping over our heads. And under the store I could make it like that, I could make it like a TV Vietnam if I screwed my eyes tight enough, black-and-white confetti under my lids, make it broken and speckled like Vietnam. And we'd blumber, we'd dead-end, we'd butt blind against those big wooden supports, until I'd hear my pap deep in my head. *"Forty-two years I worked underground, and I learnt. What kind of creak the timbers make. When it's just the ground giving. When it's gonna be a roof fall."* We played soldiers, worms, miners, dogs. People humping through the hills, hills full of people humping. And ten years later, me and Steve in the high school counselor's office, slouching, a chance to skip class, and the recruiter hooked my eyes in his and he said to me: "Son, you *look* like a Marine."

The last child-scrawly letter carried a creased photo of some little black-headed girl Kenny claimed was his wife. "Picture must be out of date," Mommy said. And after we found out he was a tunnel rat, they started pulling things from the past to make it all fit in hindsight. They would tell how he dragged out the dead cat stinking up under the house. Tell how he rescued the keys locked in the trunk at

I'd reach down and close my hand on sponge and rot, the bones stained the same yellow as the dead cornstalks there. The flattest place I've ever stood, and the land, my father would say. That's what will always be here for us. Me little and the wind passing my corduroy pants and the only thing we can count on. Raw now. Bloated deer caught up in the wash, flint-colored like the trees and the ground, and the long-ago people scattered to craziness. I gathered them.

I shiver on the porch in that unseasonable warm, my father buried in dark, just the bill of his cap and the thrust of his nose, in the smell of the drowned things rotting. I've got fingers in my pockets, I say to myself. And they're not mine. But I am quiet. It is quiet on the porch. They used to tell a lot of stories, back when my grandfather and my uncles were still around, stories that went way, way back, my people coming on this piece of ground in 1773. And my grandfather, when he was dressed and to himself and upright in his rocking chair, he used to tell a time he was fishing below the ford and spied in the silt there a musket ball lying in a little whorl. And he traced, he said, the groove it had made clear back into the bank where he saw it had rolled out of the skull of a child clutching a bone comb with its handle carved like a doll. He reburied her, my grandfather said. But after he died, the others began to wonder if it had been at all. They called it just a story, and only my father was left to swear it, him a little boy then, watching with a string of dying smallmouth bass slapping feeble against his calf. There on the bank of what the little girl would have called Wappatomaka.

In the day, from the house, they can barely see me, scudding across the Big Bottom like a piece of flood drift. Laziness, I imagine they think it is, her father's daughter, not helping and so much to be done. Dawn to sunset washing the earth away, I've carried bucket after bucket just off my bedroom floor, raising the silt out the board cracks with a scrub brush and daubing it clean. And still, of a night, the odor of the riverbed all through the house, and I sleep with it soaking my head. Before I can dig the big hole, I have to have them all heaped together, and when I've stolen the hour or two, I hide them in the furrow under the dirt. I cover them light.

Wappatomaka. They say it means white ground.

It will have to be a deep hole, an all-night-long hole, else a spring flood will unsettle them again, or the new roads, someone's summer home after we're gone. Bus bellies down into a trench and waits for me, moon half washed away by now, and though the dark spooks me in a tight place and worries me worse in a big open like this one, I dig. The earth is damp and loose and cakes in the folds of my jeans. It moves easy. But on the way down, I hit another one, him all in one piece, and then what do you do? What do you do?

Buster does not bark. I catch him out the tail of my eye, my father, coasting cross the Big Bottom like a spirit in that long underwear he sleeps in, having woke, I understand all of a sudden, in the mazey black of the house, and found even me gone. Running towards me with his hands driving open and forward, like spades, and he bellows something I hear only as a question, the end of it lifting over my head, him sleepmurky and moonblind and in his boots. And I call out, stop, stop, but he is in the loose dirt already though he does not know it, until we both hear them brickle up under his feet.

The river is still up, hishing in the riffle. Wappatomaka. They say it means white ground. I drop my shovel because I am tired, heavy with this dirt in our veins.

DIRT

This task demanded not only special skills, but also—it was recognized—a special type of temperament and courage. The tunnel rats were obliged to perform the most unnatural and stressful of tasks: to crawl through pitch-dark, narrow, low, earthen tunnels for hundreds of yards, facing the threat of sudden death at any moment. . . . In damp black holes dug for the slim and slight Vietnamese, most Americans found claustrophic panic barely controllable.—*The Tunnels of Cu Chi,* by Tom Mangold and John Penycate

Historically, young Appalachians have been disproportionately represented in the military and in combat situations. . . . Seven hundred eleven West Virginians, or 85 for every 100,000 males in the state, were killed in Vietnam, more per capita than any other state.—*Caught Up In Time: Oral History Narratives of Appalachian Vietnam Veterans,* by John Hennen

I was seven when Kenny sent the letter about what he was doing, letter on wide-ruled paper, nearly erased through in spots. Mommy slipped her cigarettes out to the side porch where she could be alone, while my daddy told me, "He was crazy before he went. Didn't take Vietnam to make him so." Then I found me a hole. I slammed out the back door and up the railroad tracks, that early spring, and the dirt soft, with the smell to it that it loses in a freeze. Hit that groundhog hole feet first at the beginning, then I pulled out and told myself, "Do like Kenny is." So I jammed my head in, then my shoulders, and at first it didn't cave, but, Lord, I was tamped tight without a thing to see, and then I heard myself screaming: "Groundhog! Groundhog!"

"Yeah, they put hillbillies down those holes along with the little Hispanics, the blacks were mostly too big. And you know they used dogs first, but they lost too many?" This was Billy Blankenship talking, several years later. "You may be right. From groundhog country we are, no doubt about that. Weasels and mushrats, beavers, snakes. Moles, rabbits, rats, there's holes just everwhere under our feet, your grandpap'll tell ya. Tunnel rats, they called em, but you may be right, more like a groundhog. A rat would of had more leeway than Kenny and them ever did, but groundhogs I imagine, fat as they are, must get plugged in terrible tight, rippling along with the flubber flattening and giving at the sides, and that's how it was. No, not rats."

Kenny left out of here when I was six and he never came back. But I remember. Running those little bottoms, hunting rabbits in the multiflora rose, the blackberry vines, brier tears in the backs of my hands. Me raggedy-lunged in the December snap, dirt clods crumbling under my feet. Yeah, I struggled to keep up with my big brother Kenny. He was my half-brother, belonged to my mother before she got married, and there was something wrong with the way he learned, and he couldn't write well so he didn't write often. His letters from Vietnam, the three of them, were like a puzzle or a secret code. Like you could hold them to a mirror and they'd make a different sense. As a kid, he would sit in closets muttering in tops of boots, that's one they tell on him. And he never did grow proper. Grandma blamed it on Mom's clothes when she was carrying him, Mommy finishing high school in a big plaid car coat with the belt cinched tight, "into April, into *May*,"

Grandma told me. Mommy kept his baby pictures in a little cedar box Dad bought her at the honeymoon at Blackwater Falls, and Kenny looked wrong even then. Like a grub, a bleached-out thing blown over with fuzz. "All the time a-arching his back when you'd try to comfert eem," my grandma said. "Never would make up to no one much."

Billy Blankenship'd been over there, too, or I'd known even less than I did. It was Kenny and Billy and Roscoe McCracken went off this creek, left the War on Poverty for the One on Communism, but just Billy came back whole. They put what was left of Roscoe in the family cemetery where he washed out in an average sort of flood two springs later, buried like he was in a low place there, but nothing came back of Kenny. I'd visit Billy Blankenship, him laid up in his modular home with the heat forever cranked too high, gnawing on storebought popcorn. "They'd treat you like a king for five dollars a day," Billy would say, his bad knee propped on a cable spool and his beans boiling, whole place reeking of salt pork and earth. "Things you could see in Patphong, oh, you can't imagine, girls picking up baht pieces off Pepsi bottles with their you-know-what's. And then there was the fish bowls." He'd always stop right there to make me ask what were those because I was twelve by that time. "Go in, got all these girls sitting behind a one-way mirror with numbers pinned on their shirts—they're watching TV and can't see you, re-member—and you pick one by her number. Like that. Fish bowls. Best year of my life, and I wasn't the only one."

"Billy! Don't be telling him that stuff." His wife, squeez-ing into her sewing factory uniform back in the bedroom. Billy did his tour in Thailand, flipped burgers in some mess hall in what you call U-bon Ratch-a-thani. Now he sat around eating storebought popcorn and spitting the hard pieces into a Hills Brothers can. Liked to take snapshots of stuff on the TV, organize them in photo albums. Stacked the albums up the sides of his chair and called them his Collection.

We snagged our war off an antenna Dad rigged in a tree, black-and-white screen and the fizzy reception. It snowed in our jungles. Holes, tunnels, dig your way to China, Alice fell through a tunnel, yeah, I liked that one. My brother dropped clear through the other side of the world. That summer after the letter we took to playing in the old Jenco store. Most of the kids stuck to the first and second floors, but me and Steve went down under. Moving like zombies in the pitch black, odor of cooped-up dirt, and the other kids thumping over our heads. And under the store I could make it like that, I could make it like a TV Vietnam if I screwed my eyes tight enough, black-and-white confetti under my lids, make it broken and speckled like Vietnam. And we'd blumber, we'd dead-end, we'd butt blind against those big wooden supports, until I'd hear my pap deep in my head. *"Forty-two years I worked underground, and I learnt. What kind of creak the timbers make. When it's just the ground giving. When it's gonna be a roof fall."* We played soldiers, worms, miners, dogs. People humping through the hills, hills full of people humping. And ten years later, me and Steve in the high school counselor's office, slouching, a chance to skip class, and the recruiter hooked my eyes in his and he said to me: "Son, you *look* like a Marine."

The last child-scrawly letter carried a creased photo of some little black-headed girl Kenny claimed was his wife. "Picture must be out of date," Mommy said. And after we found out he was a tunnel rat, they started pulling things from the past to make it all fit in hindsight. They would tell how he dragged out the dead cat stinking up under the house. Tell how he rescued the keys locked in the trunk at the Stonecoal Dam picnic, "just wormied his way right behind that back seat, deed he did." Sometimes when Billy was drunk he'd change his story entirely and pretend he'd been in Vietnam with Kenny. Croon "Cu-chi, Cu-chi," like he'd stood over the tunnels and handed Kenny burgers when he wiggled out, and I wondered if Kenny came up blackfaced as Pap. Kenny's face sloping into that no-color hair and his big hillbilly chin, I remember. Only sizeable thing on the boy, and I guess even that wouldn't hang up in a tunnel.

That's right, three off this creek went over and two came back, Billy Blankenship with a year's experience in institutional food prep and Roscoe McCracken in his box, that was 1971. The McCracken cemetery was full, everyone said so, but his mother bawled louder over Roscoe going in the town graveyard than she had over Roscoe dying, so they finally agreed to squeeze him in. Still, the only way he'd fit without shifting everybody else was tuck Roscoe in the side of the bank, and I could picture him. Scrunched up forever in the downhill corner of that coffin.

We wore church clothes for the graveside service, but no one out of Roscoe's bunch had been up that hollow for several years. And after we rattled our cars back the dirt road, we saw the only way to reach the cemetery knoll was wade the creek or drive across it. If you could call it a creek. Because someone was running cattle up in there, and it wasn't a creek anymore. It was just mess. All cow shit and swamp, hoof-puddled slime, this April and drizzling as we sat. So we finally abandoned the cars and splattered across. Poor Roscoe, they were just trying to give him a modern funeral, had the boy in a big white hearse, but the town funeral director looked once at that swamp and swore the hearse'd cross it over his own dead body. So they set all the flower arrangements out of the van, and they transferred Roscoe in where the flowers had been. The van skidded to the creek where it bogged down in two blinks, spinning and screaming and throwing the ground, and they shouldered her and they rocked her and they pried at her with fence boards. At last they yanked Roscoe out again, and ten of them, muck-freckled to their balding heads, hand carried that flag-nificent coffin to where everyone stood around the hole on a slant. But while we prayed over Roscoe, the cattle nosed around the cars and discovered the floral arrangements there. Carnations and dahlias and all manner of stuff they'd never found in a field, then they polished them off right down to the ribbons.

Kenny's picture sat on top the TV for years, him startled and midgety under his hat. Army hat like a stewpot upside down on Kenny's tiny head, that big chin looping out like a gourd. Eventually the picture traveled to the bookcase and then on to the wall of the basement stairs, but by that time Mommy, too, had passed. Held on for nine months after the diagnosis and got religion near the end, but she never gave up those cigarettes. Tempered the tar with God. Big plaid wool coat, Grandma said, and after Mommy died I learned from Billy Blankenship that it had been by her schoolbus driver that Kenny came, an older man related to the Jenco Everts. "Jenco Everts, not the Smotesfield Everts. Them Jenco Everts, they're little-boned like that, you know," Billy said. "Got the dwarfism in em," said Dad. Kenny buried under that car coat Mommy wouldn't take off, into April, into May, buckled in tight under Mommy's dress. Then a little twig-legged fellow with his own belt always wrapped a time and a half around his waist. I slept with him the first six years of my life, and he let me snug up against his back in the cold, his shoulder blades knobbing his long johns. And his skin, near see-through it was, pale,

pale, wouldn't brown, wouldn't burn. And the blue inking along under it so you could watch how he worked.

After all that trouble to put Roscoe in the right hole, he went on and rolled out two springs later when the water got up. I was at school when the McCracken cousin arrived with the bad news, but a flock of little kids came running off the ridge to meet the bus and tell us: You all missed it, Roscoe went and flopped out the ground. And I remember, believe it was the one they called Butchy. I remember clear lifting my head after stepping off the bus and seeing him come down that hill in nothing but a striped pullover shirt and his daddy's big rubber boots, them all the way up to Butchy's thighs. Butchy trying to keep up in these boots, his legs all bendy-bandy, crooking every which way, the others hooting with the holy horror of the Roscoe resurrection. And then Butchy pitching, sprawling, screaming on his belly in the jagged shale.

Yeah, we lived on a groundhog shale road, deep-rutted from the runoff. And we had groundhog shale yards, where the grass comes stubborn or not at all. And do you remember that boy we grew up with they called "Groundhog"? A roly-poly boy with oily silt-colored hair? And don't forget the groundhog song, shoulder up my ax and whistle up my dog, uh-huh, uh-huh. And the old-timers, they will tell you, the way stewed groundhog eats. Gritty greazy fat things with the flavor of dirt.

Now my dad's people were farmers, all of them, wouldn't none of them go underground, but Kenny, I reckon, took after Mom's side. Because Grandpap, he died of the dirt in his lungs, I'd heard them called black since the time I could listen, and I always wondered just how that could be. But I saw his bare chest only once. Down at that bitter creek over to their place, coppered-up with the acid, the runoff, you know, me building mud forts while he slept in the shade. I snuck over and undid his buttons easy so he wouldn't feel it and wake, me looking for that black lung shadowed on his skin.

But it was white as mine and Kenny's, and just as hairless.

I went in a groundhog hole once, did I tell you? head first even, when I was very small, and Lord God, was I tamped in tight. And at first it didn't give. Until I panicked and began to buck, and then it did cave in. The odor of earth in root and the thaw. My ears full up and dirt in my scream.

TALL GRASS

‗

She is born in tall grass there between the apple trees, them like crippled old people looking on, and the bugs looting heavy after she comes. Timothy beards sloppy with it. Their seed a dry seed. Mother fourteen years old and this when it is mostly white men work the orchard, only a few Puerto Ricans for the dirtiest jobs and no blacks, but her grandaddy watches her close, though she grows up rust-colored like the rest. A rust-speckled enamel. Sweat bees, bottle flies, wheeling away from the mess in the grass with her birth on the bottoms of their feet.

Fried sour apples and canned meat she remembers earliest, the shanty a kerosene throat gob of a winter. Come summer, she plays in the peach rot in the corner of the packing shed while her mother bags, winesaps rumbling the antiquated conveyor belt, and the women laughing full from their throats. Let's get it in high gear, this from Mister, but the women just crow, and it is only Ervin, locust husk on a high stool, who mutters and bulls. There she learns bees. Her lip stung and her crying obliterated in the ungreased gears and the apple chutter and the hoots of the women, her lip ballooning to fill the rafters. Busting past those to rub the clouds. Later, in early winter, she will squat whole afternoons in a forgotten crate along one of the orchard rows. Frost smoking mysterious off petrified grass, the grass, she sees, in clumps thrown forward, like women with fresh-washed hair, forward thrown in clumps. Heaved like that. And the deer in the distance trodding this hair tender.

Teenage 1970s and the migrants, Puerto Ricans and Jamaicans, African big-bundled heads walking rigid-backed the shoulders of the county road under the drench of an Appalachian August night sky. The brown people get shanties like hers, but the black ones are put up in abandoned schoolbuses, and the scent from the dining hall a foreign breeze so much more complicated than salt, black pepper, and pork. She stands the edge of the lot, breathes it before heading home. Thirteen, she is packing now, and Angelino rides to the shed on the flatbed behind Mister's tractor, Angelino pulling the crates, ball-muscled in his arms, and flinging fruit on the line.

Conceived, then born, she reconceives in tall grass, her Angelino kneading her between the legs, speaking surf in her face, rolls out and sprays. He has come, he tells her, across an ocean, and an ocean is something she will never see. This on Sunday afternoons, her grandaddy not letting her out after dark. Unromantic dog day sun, the grass bleached and the bees bad in their wet. Her creeping to the little creek in the hollow seam after it's done, lying full-length in knee-deep water and glad to take stones in her back. And she reworks it in her head until she reaches a point between a weeping and a come, which she will know no better than the ocean.

Her mother a grandma at twenty-seven, her own a great at forty-two. Her grandaddy has raised two generations, but balks at three, and the old man, Ervin, agrees to marry her with a television thrown in. Shocking handsome by three years old, her son is dark, curly-headed, looks like none of her people, and she calls him Angelino, but the old man calls him Karl. The old man rubs his infant skin at night with Ivory soap, wishful at making it lighter.

In the early '80s, the orchard bankrupts and the shanties are empty year-round except those of the whites who have no place to leave to. Lush apple waste, the trees untended, unthinned, but still sapping, budding, blooming, swelling, to shrivel knot-hard on branches or rot and smear in the grass. Deer ranging bold, and the yellow jackets, delirious. Her mother by now has taken up with a chicken catcher a county over and appears on holidays to straddle the front stoop and cuss the out-of-state tags driving dirt in the shanty as they pass up the hill to their new weekend homes.

The other children come rust-haired and speckled like herself. Her forced to sleep between the old man and the wall, a familiar old-people odor of stalish urine and a yeast unwashed. And her life a weight, thrown again and again, against that wall. One weekday in January she must escape the house, the little ones intolerable fussy and the wood-stove stoked like Satan. She bundles them and goes, Angelino with the three-year-old by the hand and the baby smashed across her chest, riding sidesaddle the fourth in her belly. The cloud cover is a patchy flannel, and the sun, straining from the far south, falls through in tired pieces. Above, the weekend homes castle the ridge among acres of uprooted fruit trees pitched in heaps to die. She drives her children ahead of her to an interruption in the grass. The tall grass, winter-blond and humped, abruptly close-cropped and brittle. A lawn. Mama, can we see inside?

Finding a chunk of limestone smaller than her fist, she shatters a rear window, bloodying her knuckles a bit.

Works out the shards with her coat doubled over her arm, and then she boosts her Angelino through. He meets them at the front door and every footfall on the plush rug is a gasp, a pleasure, under a gallery of self-photographs the second-homers have hung. The chocolate pie they discover in the refrigerator is missing only one piece. She feeds them from a single spoon, deciding dirtying more would be bad manners, while each weekend face beams from the wall. And between turns, her babies wallow, luxurious, in the cream carpet.

SISTER

Mason'd come in the still-dark and dress me over my
nightgown, it bunched up under my pants and the odor of
damp wool scarf in my mouth. Pale rings of wrist between
last-year's sleeves and the mud-colored gloves Santa gave
the free-lunch kids, ticking: have you been a good little
girl, a good little girl, a good little girl. My brother worked
rough without meaning it, jerked me near to lace my
boots, and with my face in his shoulder I could smell the
weeks-old blood in his coat, the animal hair. Quiet, I kept
quiet, like he told me. Across the room, Cill's bed was not
speaking. As he led me down the steps, I'd push my hand
against the black, dad, grandma, mom, Cill, exhaling
heavy circles of sleep, choking up around us like a draw-
string on a sack until Mason'd break them with a clatter.
Fist of bullets dropped in his pocket. That was the winter
Mason never left me home without him. The winter I was
witched.

Frost lay on the grass. It crackled when we crossed it to
the tracks, a skiff of ice bleached every tie, and when I
drew air, I felt my insides whiten up. I felt them brittle as
the stalks of brush along the rails. I could keep up good,

Mason said so, and it would be yet night when we'd meet
the other two at the cattle crossing. Jess, the blank of his
face broken by freckles the size of tacks, and strange, slow
Buddy, stumbling along with his mouth slung open, spinning great ghosts of breath against the dark. By the time
we reached the fencerow there was some sun trying. Some
starved, some struggly sun, and when the deer came, they
came all of a sudden, like spilled ink. Darkening a field
straining to come light. Mason and Jess'd take turns,
Buddy no shot at all, and after Jess fired, the buck
streamed on for a few hundred feet before he stuttered,
foundered on his knees, drove himself back up with his
hindquarters, and pushed to the black lip of the woods.
Hit eem again, Jess told Mason, quiet, and my brother
raised his rifle and dropped him through the neck. I
watched the does pour over the bob wire and soak back
into the face of the mountain.

Now there was light enough to see how the night had
rimed the corn stubble, to see the river smoking slow and
deliberate. We walked up on him leery, but he seemed full
dead without enough antler to threaten us if he wasn't, and
as Jess opened him, he spilled his smoke into that of the
river. His heart shut down like a stone dropped in a pool of
standing water, last pulse shivering through the tangle of
guts. They left most of them to steam in the dead stalks,
carried the heart and liver back in a plastic bread bag.
Stout Buddy dragged the carcass to the crosstree they'd
rigged from a bit of railroad trestle over the slough, they
worked quick and I was home in time to catch the bus to
school. Where the teacher had me sitting too near the heat
register and I nodded off on the greasy desktop, so many
times that winter she stopped waking me.

In the evening, we'd eat. All that beauty and we'd put it
inside us.

SISTER

* * *

That winter I tended toward close spaces. Behind the couch, the blanket chest, full closets. Under a bed, I watched my grandmother pull herself hand over hand toward the bathroom, nursing those great legs along. Them blooming brilliantly, scarlets, violets, turquoise, pink, dazzling under her sallow housedress. Butt ends forced into white bobby socks. Soles dirtied black. Later, I heard her grope near the hall closet. She keened over and over two lines of a hymn (That saaaved a-uh wreeetch), and light rushed on top of me, carrying her odor in it. Her sweating year round under the burden of the legs, and she never had gotten used to a house like ours, a house with a shower in it. When she saw me in the closet, she barked once before she lost her wind. What's (uh-huuhh) a matter (uh-huuhh) with you? And Cill, coming up behind her, said, She has bad dreams. Looking our grandma full in the face.

And she didn't know I was behind the couch that other afternoon when she was watching her story on the TV, but I couldn't help the sneeze. That swollen bulk rearing round, eyes runny, eyes two yellow blisters, wheezing, All the time (uh-huuhh) carrying on (uh-huuhh) like you're (uh-huuhh) afflicted. She coughed like she was bringing her lungs up her throat. Get out from behind this sofa. She had there laid open on the cushion a handkerchief of hard candy, clotted up with the heat of her body and smelling of her. She carried it all the time. And I wondered if she was going to holler to my father, but instead she fixed those blisters on me, and she said,

Did I tell you about that little girl who was witched around here a few months back? Yeah. Milksnakes got her.

67

* * *

Cill and Mason took me when they went, up the dirt road to Jess's, Jess's house like a picture house, white all around and ten steps to the porch. But we never climbed them because Jess'd be out, Buddy behind, as soon as we'd reach the yard, and he'd latch all five of us in the barn. Barn long-time empty, a skim of horse scent still pooling over the stalls. The dogs slept there burrowed in the stale hay. The two males, mongrels, slouch-hipped and rangy, and the bitch, Jess's pride, a Black and Tan purebred, sleek as a catfish. They claimed they had papers on her said Clandeston Dale's Black Rose, but what they called her was Sister. And she knew how to bell the hills, them running coons above our house at night.

I'd take her there between my arms and I'd trace her skull, the folds of her neck, each knoll along her spine. I'd lay my face in the hollow of Sister's flank. Buddy stretched out easy on his side, blocky glasses bound to his head with an elastic band, one ear snugged up to the radio that never carried batteries, the other ear turned to me, its channels seamed with dirt. And I listened tight, but could not hear what Buddy did. The others besides Buddy made plans, and the sounds they spoke followed the tendons that wrenched Jess's throat. A plucked wire. Jess, even his lips mottled, his eyelids, spade of earth pitched over his head. Jessie was the maddest.

* * *

You know about milksnakes, don't ya? my grandma said.

I knew they thieved milk, sucked cows' tits before the farmer got up in the morning. I'd seen one in our own

shed, even barn-colored it was. Colored like dried cow shit
walked to a powder.

Milksnakes'll witch ye. Instermints of Satan.

A bead of red candied saliva globed up in the corner of
her mouth.

What I heard about this recent little girl was she was acting all peculiar, hiding around the house and sneaking out
early every morning, and they wouldn't of thought so
much about it except she was wearing Sunday School
clothes. This a Wednesday, a Thursday. So they decided to
hide there in the weeds and watch her. They saw her come
out the house about sunrise in them church clothes, shoes
buckled on the wrong feet, and saw she was carrying something, real careful, between her hands, saw it was a chinee
bowl—believe they said red roses painted round the rim—
and they said she carried that thing on up toward their
shed, them sneaking along behind her. They watched her
carry it through the lot, her feet finding the way for them
hypnotized eyes. Then she opened the shed door and they
saw the milksnake, coiling itself out the sill there. And she
put down her bowl—milk, bread tore up in it, they said—
like it was an offering, yessir, like an offering, and old milksnake slid over and drank out it. Just like that. And when
he was finished—his belly swoled up like he'd swallowed a
little baby robin, you know—what do you think she did?

I didn't know.

Knelt down in the dirt and sucked up what that snake
left.

*   *   *

Then, in the barn, Cill'd start to cry, just a little, and they'd
shut up their plans, quit arguing the when and the where,

69

and they waited. Jess'd put an arm around her, their bodies
darkening a place in the winter light through the barn wall,
and he riffled his fingers across her hair. Mason knuckled
the mongrels' heads. Buddy with his radio. They waited.

What was it to be witched? Did you make things happen, or did they happen to you? Was it this bad, running in
me gummy, plugged solid from my chest to my back? The
door opening in the early night and the cranking across the
room. This need to duck down and be hidden.

The mutts, yeah, they'd tree a coon, but you could hear
the beagle in their bray, "nYaaa, nYaaa, nYaaa, nYaaa"
while Sister's breath was pure. "Ahh-ooooo. Ahh—ooooo.
Ahh-ooooo," Sister sang me, and the noise she crooned, it
ran the ridgelines. This was the noise the mountains'd make
if they could thrum themselves, this beauty in her voice. But
they kept mute, the mountains did. Until Jess fired across
them, the shot ricocheting from face to face, and the dogs
cried once or twice, dampened. I watched the purple behind
my eyelids. It blossomed like my grandma's legs. The bedroom door opened so quiet I wouldn't have known at first
except for the draft. The springs across the room gave their
first grieved groan. What was it to be witched?

* * *

Then my grandma picked that linty clump of hardtack off
her hanky and worked the whole mess into her mouth.
Ground off what she wanted, spit back the better part of it
on the couch for later.

Who was that little girl, I said, not able to help it.

Can't tell you that, she said, sucking her candy smooth
like she did to keep it from being so rough on her gums,
Can't tell you that, but I'll tell you this. People what's
witched don't remember the witching after it's done.

My mama passed through the front door, told me she needed me in the kitchen, and I followed her, the bad rising in me like a vomit. I followed my mama, hung together with wires she was, her face ground down around its bones, but there was no food smell in the kitchen, just a cigarette smoldering on a saucer in the dim.

What was your grandma talking about? she said.

I don't know, I said, telling the truth. I sat over the saucer and tasted the tobacco smoke, this the scent of my mama. I drew the smoke out of the air, the smell of my mama, a comforting thing. Then I looked up at the cupboard, the set of good china that we used at Christmas, Thanksgiving. Pink roses painted round the rims. Mama, my chest hurts, I said, and she stubbed out her cigarette.

Honey, she said, you know I got nothing for that.

* * *

I didn't go straight home after school. Jess and Buddy were at the railroad crossing when me and Cill got off the bus. Jess, that long muddy hair running in buckling breaks like a river that's got too high, and Buddy squatted at his feet, working serious a half stick of beef jerky. Beside him there in the cinders and broken bottles lay a plastic air rifle with a splintered stock. Cill got in the truck with Jess and told me go on home, Mason is there. I watched them out of sight, then I followed Buddy away from the house.

I let him keep a good bit ahead, not easy with listening to him talk the way he did. Something he heard in that radio and repeated to the broom sage along the bank. He carried his air rifle the way we'd been taught to carry true guns, and by the time I broke out of the woods to the clearing, by the time I stood over the slough, he was already on the fencerow, sighting that broken rifle on some nothing across the burnt-out field. The land a husk. This brittle, this mustard-colored winter. I dropped on my knees and rested my face between the trestle ties, and I pulled air into the place in my chest where I carried the rocks. The litter of hides, of heads, the scattered forelegs, odorless in this kind of cold. The foamy sky squatted near and damp, a wheezy, a cold like a press.

The dump was a little ways beyond, folded between the tracks and the county road, and someone had just pulled over. Plastic bags unraveled midair to shower garbage in the creek. When the truck spun out, the sun rolled free of the clouds, and it fired the shattered bottles, the chrome of the refrigerators and stoves, the windshields of the junked cars piggybacked under the road, stunning me. Then the sky emptied except for the wood smoke scrolling off the mountain, the wood smoke rising off Jess's roof, the house itself screened in the crosshatch of naked trees. There was a little girl found in a refrigerator like this one up near Mouth of Seneca, suffocated dead, and I'd picture her sometimes while I lay across the room listening to Cill's bed squeak. I saw her monkey-eyed, curled like a spring, arms and legs shrunk up. The refrigerator door hung open. I climbed in. I just wanted to see, for a minute, how it felt to be that shriveled girl, sealed tight in a box. The refrigerator started to topple back. Easy and slow. Until I could see the sky above me, emptied, its only interruption the wood smoke rising off the top of Jess's house. The door swinging to, easy and slow, shutting it off gentle, that smoke rising off the top of Jess's house, and I lay quietly on my back. Mason had a copperhead in a pickle jar full of formaldehyde. It was the only interest he'd ever taken in school. I wrapped my arms around myself.

The ground hissed. Somebody waded cinders off the tracks and down the embankment. I heard him at the

electric stove next the refrigerator, metal grating on the
burners, the clicking of the knobs. A grocery list in forced
soprano, Get-me-some-beans-some-bacon-a-six-pack-a-
choclit-Yoo-Hoo. He rapped on the refrigerator door like he
wanted to ask me for supper. When I didn't answer, he
opened it, face gridded off by those blocky glasses. He
poked me around the stomach with the broken butt of his
gun, and after I climbed out, he mumbled a message to some
nobody through the transistor he carried in his CPO jacket.

Walking home, he turned around, said, You seen it, ain't
ya? ain't ya? but I didn't know what he meant. You seen it
before, ain't ya? He giggled or sobbed, his face away from
me. Me and Jess'll take cur of eem. We'll take cur of eem.
The wood smoke coiled off the top of Jess's house. What
was it to be witched?

* * *

That night Cill's bed woke me again, the bed talking in its
sleep. I held my breath. The bed rose, a shriek, the shriek
lifting, dropping, lifting. I lost my breath and found it
again just as the dogs up the hill caught hold the trail.
"nYaaa, nYaaa, nYaaa, nYaaa," and over top that, Sister,
her lungs outgrown that cramped beagle bray, Sister
busted it loose, ringing, "Ah-ooooo! Ah-ooooo! Ah-
ooooo!"

But the dogs weren't running the ridge tonight. They
were bearing down the hollow towards the house. Cill's
bed all moan, and our own dog, Max, barking now from
under the back porch. Sister returned it, so near I looked
toward the window behind Cill's bed despite myself. The
bed springs heaved once more. Then they were still. Max,
scared to come out from under the back porch, carried on
like some crazy screwed in a jar.

Cill's bed tore in two. A panting black mass rose off the mattress, a darker place in the darkened room. My father drifted out the door. When he was gone, I ran to the window and smeared the steam with the flat of my hand, but I saw nothing. Max bawled under the back porch. I heard Sister and the others all on top of each other, so it sounded, they'd been tied now and rushed against their collars, and I looked over my shoulder to where Cill sat upright in her quiet bed, her hands folded in her lap. When I turned back to the window, Jess's flashlight was trickling between the trees. Then a box of light fell out the kitchen window where I knew my mother and father must be, scaredycat Max carrying on under the back porch, and Sister and the mongrels broke out of the woods. They were strangling themselves, hurling their bodies against their leads, and behind them wobbled the eye of the flashlight. Only Sister still carried the game scent in her muzzle, still singing, "Ah-oooo! Ah-ooooo! Ah-ooooo!" The others were just barking. I left the bedroom while Cill sat upright, glazed against her headboard.

Hacking up her lungs in the next room, my grandma wheezed at me, comeinhelpmeupwhatsgoingon, but through the other door, I saw Mason lying still. I lit down the stairs to the kitchen where my mother hunched over the kitchen sink peering through the window, puddled dark under her eyes. She turned to my father, she said, Jee-sus, Macy. Jee-sus. My father's shoulders hackled. Boom of belly slung over the band of his long-john bottoms, and the blood bolted into his face as Jess screamed my father's name. The name lifting and dropping over the mutts' and Max's and Sister's steady song. My mother wafted toward the back door in her raggy nightgown, and I dragged myself up over the sink to the window she'd left, the rocks working their way, sharp, between my ribs. I watched the sliver of light fall on the back porch, the kitchen light spread from the kitchen door, gradual. Jess was sobbing now. He'd scream himself empty then stop to gulp air, and I heard my mama call something out before she opened the door, something that was mauled in the roar. But Jess wanted to see my father so bad it *was* my father Jessie saw, edging out onto the porch. When Buddy raised his gun and the shot sprayed, I saw Sister rear on her hind legs. I saw her dance in her chain.

* * *

Rock me. Rock me. The hollow rocked me (she was narrow). It was a tight hollow without a name and a stony run in the bottom of it. Like the lap of a woman kneeling.

My mama had stuttered backwards, the way a wounded buck'd struggle for trees, then she sat hard on the floor in the living room. Her right arm bloodied her nightgown.

It was the dogs found me, an hour after I'd run. Buried in the leaves, crusty with frost. They pushed their noses against my cheeks, delighted to see me laid low like that, they treated me with their tongues. Rock me. Buddy came up behind them, whispering into the brush. I watched him pull a fistful of pine needles and crush them between his palms. Cup his hands over his face and draw breath. At first he didn't see me at the bottom of the hounds, then he called them away in words I'd never heard and picked me up, Sister pawing his thigh to nuzzle me. Rock me.

Buddy was stout. He carried me home. The winter I was witched.

BAIT

≡

They would have gotten down to the highway sooner, but Mom wouldn't let Thomas turn on his scanner before seven o'clock, and although Carrie had heard the sirens, she didn't wake him. A week ago, she would have, and they would have been there in time to see the bodies pulled clear, but this week Carrie didn't want to see bodies coming out of anywhere. Thomas charged down the dirt road ahead of her, stumbling and nearly falling once before rescuing himself in a spectacular kind of skip. Carrie let her uncle Thomas go. Now she could see the sheriff along with some state police she didn't know, and then Shorty who drove the tow truck, and finally, a half-grown yellow dog that hurled itself over and over again at the sheriff's leg. The sheriff, over and over again, chopped it down with the kind of inattention you might give the snapping of green beans during a TV show. Each time he was knocked backwards, the dog would bunch up his haunches and lunge again, his tongue whipping around like a pink bandanna.

Thomas had pulled up to the border of this self-important little group, his legs splayed out like the other men's and his hands hooked in the back of his pants, and his head, flat on his shoulders with no more interruption of a neck than a groundhog has, swiveling back and forth to follow the voices. He had his First Aid kit planted between his tennis shoes. Carrie sighed and hooked her own arm into Thomas's to drag him across the double yellow line to the bait stand, Thomas muttering a little in protest. At last the sheriff caught the yellow dog with a violent cuff that toppled him, yelping, onto his spine. When he righted himself, he spurted across the highway to where Nuppleholt reclined in his lounge lawn chair in front of his bait stand. He was Nuppleholt's pup, of course, and due to certain slickish tendencies he had demonstrated in earliest puppyhood, Nuppleholt had named him after a certain ubiquitous governor.

"Roads'll get a few," Nuppleholt announced in his philosophical tone upon their arrival. "Yeah, the roads can getcha." He paused to drop a gob of snuffy saliva into a Grape Fanta can. "My word of rest, this Route 50. Dropped down on top the state like a big old pile of pig intestines." Stroking Archie's belly with the sole of his boot as a reward for courting the sheriff's calves, he eyed Thomas. "Gotta watch him today?" he asked Carrie.

"Yeah. Mom got some work in town. Who wrecked?"

"Oh, nobody you know. Coupla boys from over in Tucker County. Don't know what they were doing up here so early of a morning."

"Heard on the scanner neither of 'em got killed."

"Well, no, not kilt dead, but pretty badly boogered up. Yeah, pretty badly boogered up, I would say."

Nuppleholt was related to them in some tangled-up bymarriage sort of way, and he got a check, disability, for putting out his back in the pulpwood. He hired Carrie on for the summer at two dollars an hour as what he called a favor to her mom, but Carrie knew it was worth way more than two dollars an hour to him to be able to lay in that lounge lawn chair all day and boss her around. She sagged into her own seat on top of the ice chest on the other side of the bait-stand door and dropped her chin into her hands in despair. The wrecker was pulling out with a mufflerless flatulence that Nuppleholt saluted with a single finger.

"See the blood?" Nuppleholt asked, and Carrie froze. It would be just like Nuppleholt to figure out how to eavesdrop on her thoughts. Then she remembered. She hadn't noticed any blood on the pavement, but it was sprayed across the inside of the windshield where it had dried in misshapen beads like muddy raindrops.

"Whole thing reminds me of that Baltimoron who bought a 'farmette' out of Ralph Landes's old home place and had the pig wreck," Nuppleholt said. "Did you hear about that?"

He had told her less than a week ago, but Carrie knew saying yes wouldn't make any difference.

"Yeah," Nuppleholt said, "this out-of-stater, Ferdinan Remington believe they said his name was, decided he was gonna put up some fence on a Sunday, and he went over to Richard Pyles's to buy him cheap some ole bob wire Richard had laying around. He had him a pickup and all, what goes with a 'farmette,' I guess, and he had his boy, a big boy, riding in the bed of the truck with this bob wire.

"Well, I believe they said it was right past the Mount Zion church when he heard a couple thuds in the back of the truck, but about that same time, he saw in front of him one of them little Vietnamese pigs, so he slammed on his brakes."

Nuppleholt was referring to one of the more bizarre forms of fallout from the Eastern Seaboard's most recent infatuation with their region: the abandoning in their hills of Vietnamese potbellied pigs that people in the suburbs

had gotten bored with, the life span of the pigs, unfortu-
nately, longer than the pig fad. The phenomenon was first
discovered when Ronnie Roach shot what he believed to
be a wild boar up on Lost Mountain and tried to check it
in as such with the Department of Natural Resources.
Since that time, it had gotten so bad they had set up a
Vietnamese potbellied pig orphanage in Martinsburg, but
Martinsburg was seventy miles away, so that didn't help
their county much. In the meantime, the displaced pigs
roamed the ridges, rooting and reproducing, raiding garbage and gardens and making a general nuisance of
themselves.

"Now what he didn't know," Nuppleholt went on,
"didn't know the thuds he'd heard behind him was the
mama of that little one, plus the rest of the litter, jumping
off the bank overhead. You know how steep it is in there.
Just tried to cross the road at the wrong time and landed
smack in the bed of that truck with the big boy and the
bob wire. And when this Ferdinan slammed on his
brakes, threw out the boy and the sow and the bob wire
and the shoats, too. Sow flies out first, then that big boy
comes a-sailing outta there and lands right on top the
mama. Pig pops like a big ole blood blister. What a mess,
they said. Thought the boy was dead at first, but it was
just pig's blood. 'Course, the sow was kind of finished.
And meantime the little ones had all run off tangled up in
the bob wire. They carried that whole roll of bob wire off
with 'em into the woods someplace, and can't nobody
find em."

Nuppleholt paused to visualize the litter, a couple of
months older now, still all strung together by the barbed
wire, the wire embedded in their hides where they had
grown up around it. The piglets floated the woods in a
kind of synchronized trot until they finally got hung up

someplace, ate everything their little snouts could reach, then starved to death. Eight carcasses flapping on a wire.

Carrie had made no response.

"Working on a Sunday." Nuppleholt provided the moral. "'Farmette.' Hah."

Cross-legged in the bait-stand turnaround, Thomas neatened up his First Aid kit, a white shoebox with a big red cross lipsticked over the lid and a rubber band to hold it together. Rowed up tidy inside lay loose Band Aids, a broken thermometer, some mysterious ointment in a brittle tube, and an Ace bandage that stunk of sweat. Nuppleholt watched him.

"What's he up to now?"

"Thinks he works for the Rescue Squad," Carrie said. *Sure, it'll come today,* her brain was whispering. *It's the worry is holding it in, worry can do that to you. Just stop worrying and it will come.*

"Well, I'll tell you, he's gonna get in trouble with that game warden bullshit. You hear me, Thomas? He's gonna ask somebody from away from here who don't know he's mental for a fishing license and get cracked upside the head with a beer bottle." Thomas was absorbed in coiling the Ace bandage. Archie padded over, snuffled at it, lost interest, padded away. Nuppleholt turned to Carrie. "Guess you ain't been watching him close enough again."

"He's not a game warden anymore," she said.

Thomas as game warden had been a year-long phase in a ten-year history of Thomas as Patrol Boy, then Thomas as State Trooper, next Thomas as Game Warden, and, most recently, Thomas as Rescue Worker. Carrie, who'd had the responsibility of keeping an eye on her uncle since she was four years old and he was fourteen, had gotten in the worst trouble with the Game Warden gig. For that one, Thomas had dressed up in a cowboy hat, mold-colored like the troopers wore, that Mom had given him during the State Police spell, and he'd even unearthed somewhere in the house an expired and laminated Pennsylvania driver's license that had belonged to Carrie's father while he was working in Pittsburgh. And away Thomas escaped, down to the river to check for fishing licenses. Most people who didn't know him just stared, but a few actually understood and either produced a license or lied that they had left it in their car. This was all last summer and fall, because the Game Warden lost interest with nothing to do after deer season, and in the meantime, Carrie got beat with an old Hot Wheels track for letting him get away. By that time, Carrie was thirteen and occupied with fantasies of her own.

Thomas had converted to Rescue Worker just this spring when they launched the Jaws of Life fundraiser. Jaws of Life were some sort of giant pliers that ripped cars open like a can opener so the rescuers could drag out bodies before they burned. Word got around that all the neighboring counties already had a Jaws of Life, a real disgrace for their own county, especially since Highway 50—what the nation called the asphalt-covered deer run that corkscrewed across the state—distinguished them with one of the highest vehicular death rates in America. So the Rescue Squad set up their roadblocks, begging donations with cut-off bleach bottles, then there were the chicken barbecues that Mom faithfully patronized while Thomas surveyed the ambulances and equipment. And soon Thomas contrived the shoebox from stray items he found around the bathroom. Mom permitted it in relief because she couldn't think of anything her baby brother could do independently in this new role. It was only appropriate for a wreck and he'd never hear about one unless people were already there who could keep him away from it.

Now Nuppleholt's first customer was pulling in, maneuvering his station wagon around Thomas in the gravel. He opened his door and without even glancing at Carrie or Nuppleholt first, got out, rested his arms on top the car window, and studied the tear in the weeds where the wreck had been.

"Who wrecked?" he said.

"Oh, nobody you all know," said Nuppleholt. "Old man and old woman from over in Preston County. Trying to get to Virginia where their little granddaughter's in the hospital. Holes in her heart."

"Heard in town they weren't killed," the regular said. He wore a pair of gold-rimmed mirror sunglasses repaired at one wing with a neat little gold safety pin.

"No, not dead," Nuppleholt said. "But pretty boogered up."

"50," was all the regular said. He bowed his head in a prayerful attitude. "How about a dozen nightcrawlers?"

"Sure," Nuppleholt said, cocking his chin at Carrie.

Carrie blew breath out of her cheeks in a victimized exhale before she trudged back into the little shed, but no one noticed. The odor of the minnows dying in their styrofoam cups brought her Cheerios up into her throat. As she filled a Shedd's Spread tub with dirt and worms, she rubbed her thighs back and forth, hopeful that some stickiness might have shown up in the last thirty minutes. But the only wetness was the white film the worms left on her hands. Little tears burned into her eyes. She squinted them back. When she came out of the building, the regular was in the middle of one she already knew.

"—and they were all riding around up there on the Rig Road, drunk, stealing people's lawn ornaments and throwing them in the back seat, but one they stoled was this big cement lion—"

"I heard it was a turtle," Nuppleholt interrupted.

"Lion, turtle," the regular continued, "whatever it was, it was big and cement. Anyway, they were taking that curve in front of Pete Willey's chicken house when they run off the road, and that big cement lion came flying forward. Hit the one boy in the back of the head and that was all she wrote."

Nuppleholt wagged his head. "Stealin' lawn ornaments," he said. "Well, I'll tell ya. The roads'll getcha."

"Closed coffin," the regular concluded.

The nightcrawler man paid Nuppleholt and lurched away with an ominous flapping noise under his hood. Lifting the Grape Fanta can to his ear, Nuppleholt sloshed it a little to calculate how full it was, then finessed another ball of saliva through the hole. Carrie crouched on the ice chest, sympathizing with the crushed McDonald's wrappers in the road.

"Hey there, Bendy," Nuppleholt said all of a sudden, addressing a waving hand he had spotted in a big F-10 pickup. Carrie drew her shoulders up around her ears. Now she'd be subjected to Nuppleholt's daily commentary on passers-by.

"I met Bendy's little niece up there to the house last week. Visiting in from Warrenton. Real short, about like that," he said, holding his hand a foot off the ground. "Runt. And she's got this one front tooth, new tooth, right here in the middle of her mouth. The mother says they're gonna pull that one out and put two new ones up there."

An orange Ford Fiesta putted past. "Wonder where Blanche's off to? You know her boy got killed in that turn over at the auction. Been years ago." He thought a while. "Buried him in his car. Now that's a true story!"

And then, "There goes Roger. He's drunk most of the time. But he keeps his car clean."

After Roger vanished, a customer Nuppleholt didn't much care for shuddered around the curve in the county's last road-faring Vega five-speed two-door. The driver was waiting for his cataracts to get bad enough to be removed, and he nearly parked right on top of Thomas until Carrie screamed, Thomas hurtled over the bank, and the First Aid kit spewed all over the gravel. Thomas's morning work was ruined. Nuppleholt shut one eye, peered with the other into his can. He noticed how it looked like a good strong ice tea.

"Who was it wrecked?" the old man demanded.

"Oh, nobody you know," Nuppleholt said. "Two kids from down in the southern part of the state. Heading off to Ocean City for their honeymoon. Drunk already."

The old man screwed up his eyebrows at Nuppleholt. "I heard in town it was two fellas work over at Abex in Winchester. One of 'em Guy Eberly's second cousin."

"Then why'd you ask?" Nuppleholt said.

"Dead?" the old man said.

"No, not kilt," said Nuppleholt. "But badly boogered up."

The old man fixed his cataracts on Carrie like he was going to learn her a real lesson. "You know they call a cop on 50 a waste because the road cleans up after herself. A driver who pushes the speed limit for over a mile on 50 is a driver who's dead." He nodded for emphasis, then shifted back to Nuppleholt. "Did I ever tell you what happened to my wife's brother's stepson when he was a kid over in Mineral County?"

"You may have," Nuppleholt said. He directed a snuff jet at the Vega's tail light, but the customer couldn't see it.

"Well," the old man went on anyway. "My wife said her brother said his stepson said when they was a-growing up over in one of them real bad turns right up against the road there, he said, said one Saturday night they was all asleep

84

and there was a big truck went off the road right across from the house.

"Said he thought he heard something, some kind of moaning and help me and carrying on, so my wife said he said he got out of bed and found the driver over the bank there, trapped in his cab, said. Said he fought that door from the outside and said the truck driver fought it from the inside, but couldn't neither one of em budge it. Driver burnt up, said.

"Said next day they found claw marks in the window glass where he'd tried to scratch his way out. And after that my wife's brother's stepson starting having nightmares, said something clawing his eyes out, from behind, said, not on the eyeball, but from behind, said, like from inside of his head, see what I'm saying?

"Well, said he never was the same after that. And has the scratchy pain in his eyes still, sometimes he does, from behind, you know.

"Seems to me he has to take some kinda drops for it.

"Anyway, that's what my wife's brother said he said. Said his stepson said, I mean."

"Yep," Nuppleholt said. "That'd do it. Roads'll getcha. One way or another."

"Got any helgramites yet?" the old man asked.

"Nope. But got some minnies back there and some real nice nightcrawlers."

"Well," the old man said, "really just wanted the helgramites. Got some bacon that'll do, I guess."

Nuppleholt shrugged, and then Thomas lumbered over to contribute his two cents.

"Wummm wummm woo mmm," the old man heard him say.

And "hm oys wum wooped up um," Nuppleholt heard him say.

"What's he talking about?" Nuppleholt asked Carrie.

"Says the sheriff said them boys in the pickup got their faces chopped up some," Carrie translated.

"Knew that," Nuppleholt said.

"What's he mean?" the old man asked.

"Hmmm wmmm ummm oo ummm," he heard Thomas say.

"Just got chopped up some," Carrie repeated.

The old man grunted back into his Vega and waved them goodbye.

"Knew we didn't have no helgramites," Nuppleholt said. "Too cheap to buy anything and just wanted in on the story." Thomas stood up with his First Aid kit, which he had reconstructed during the talk, and stumbled down over the bank where he began rooting around in the weeds.

"Why can't Thomas be something useful, like a garbage man?" Nuppleholt asked.

By this time, Archie was laid out in the napping pose he assumed on the hottest of days, balanced on his backbone with his four legs cocked up and dangling at the paw joints. Gnats orbited Carrie's head like microscopic vultures. A pulpwood truck rumbled past, and Carrie, reminded of a movie where the hero had saved himself from Nazis by clinging to the underneath of a truck chassis, pictured herself fleeing the state on the underbelly of that one. Nuppleholt pried the lid off his snuff can and prodded around the edges with his little finger. "Looks like you're gonna have to run down to the store and pick me up some more Gold River. I'll keep an eye on him for you," he added, shifting an elbow in the direction of Thomas.

With a tortured sigh that Nuppleholt ignored, Carrie heaved herself off the ice chest, accepted the money without looking at him, and plodded away down the shoulder.

Every few minutes she had to stop to shake shale out of her white sandals. A tractor trailer blew by, hooting its horn and driving the roadside litter into a little tornado around Carrie's shins, and she threw her finger in the direction of the receding rearview mirror. *Now if Ajames,* the friendly part of her brain whispered, *is right there across from that sumac, that means you're not.*

Ajames was Archie's older half-brother, black instead of yellow, and he had been run over last winter, but Nuppleholt hadn't bothered to bury him, which Carrie thought indecent. She had followed Ajames' decay for months, the corpse flattening and rotting away in a holey and haphazard manner until he now reminded her of a funnel cake or a loosely braided black rug. Carrie drew up parallel with the sumac and peered over the bank. Ajames was nowhere to be seen. Carrie's insides dropped from an already very low point somewhere between her hips and knees on down towards her ankles. Eventually spying Ajames some ten yards farther on, she changed tactics.

This is the last one, God, she prayed. *Your last chance to let me know. If I get to the bridge without getting another rock in my shoe, I'm not.*

She trod gingerly now, picking up each sandal and laying it down gentle, and she oozed perspiration from every pore, but she was beginning to feel she might make it when, suddenly, another car appeared. It honked in a cheerful fashion and fluttered with hands, and she recognized it as some kids from the high school and waved back, flattered, because she was only in junior high. She turned completely around to watch them go, wondering if they would have picked her up if they'd been going in her direction, so it wasn't until she set off again that she realized she'd picked up a piece of shale in her sandal during the distraction. The little bridge was still some fifty steps away.

Well, that was it. She was going to have to tell him.

He was eighteen years old, already graduated and with a job in the store, but her being in junior high hadn't mattered to him at all as he slid Nuppleholt's Gold River across the counter in such a way that he could fondle her hand. And if the manager wasn't around, he might even sneak her some gum. Day after day, bored senseless on the ice chest, she relived the way she had woken up all under her skin every time she'd climbed in the front seat of his pickup with him, not even touching him, no, her clear on the far side of the cab and still the current brightening up her blood. And that boy could handle Route 50 like a roller coaster. She would meet him at the bottom of their road after supper, Nuppleholt long gone and the bait stand locked up with all the bait creatures doing their dying inside. Then him and Carrie would run the roads, burning up the straights, bobsledding those deadly curves, until he'd jerk the wheel abruptly onto some side road and bury them back in the brush. Every time they went, he took another base, until he was straining at home and let it be known no score meant he wouldn't play anymore. She reasoned she was in love and once wouldn't matter anyway. And that time even his cap fell off, onto the pickup floor, and she realized that that was the last part of his body she saw bare. The crown of his head.

Now that she was sure, she was going to have to tell him, and he wasn't going to want to hear it, no, not one bit. Especially since, as far as she could tell, he had broken up with her, which she had to assume from the fact that the only words he had spoken to her in the last eleven and a half days were the counting back of her change. As the store came into view, she collapsed deeper into despair. She was soaked now, and stinky, she felt sure, around the armpits, and that wasn't going to work in her favor at all.

But it wasn't him at the counter. It was a boy named Lonnie Peeler with a face the color and pitted texture of a pancake telling you it's time to flip it. She stole a glance towards the back of the aisles to doublecheck, then stepped up to ask for Nuppleholt's Gold River.

Lonnie waggled a disk of snuff at her between his thumb and forefinger. "Tell Nuppleholt look what we just got in," he said. He paused for suspense. "Cherry-flavored Copenhagen."

Carrie ignored this. "Nuppleholt rubs Gold River," she said. Despite herself, she glimpsed the rubbers they kept on a little wire rack behind the counter where you had to ask for them. A man caressed a beautiful woman in a protective way, her eyes slanting back towards him admiringly. He had told her rubbers were only necessary if she was having her period.

"And a pack of Virginia Slims," she added nonchalantly.

"Ha," Lonnie said. "*You* ain't eighteen."

"So," she said. "I know where I can get 'em."

"Then go get 'em," Lonnie said. She pocketed Nuppleholt's snuff and gave the store a last once-over.

"I know who you're looking for," Lonnie said.

"You wish," she answered.

"He ain't coming in til three o'clock," Lonnie said. "Hey, who was it wrecked over there this morning?"

"Nobody you know." She wanted to wheel on her heels for a dramatic exit, but Lonnie held hostage Nuppleholt's change.

"You hear about those Satan worshipers wrecked over in the Narrows last month?" He didn't consider his coworker much to look at, and this boosted his own confidence. "The survivors are supposed to sacrifice a little blonde-headed blue-eyed boy!" A manager emerged from the back, Carrie stuck out her palm in an assertive manner, and Lonnie was forced to return the change. "Some people so scared they won't even let their kids play outside!" he was calling as she escaped out the door.

Ha, Carrie thought. Putting the most interesting part about the sacrifice right there at the beginning. Lonnie Peeler couldn't even tell a story right.

At some distance from the bait stand, she could see that Nuppleholt had joined Archie's nap, Nuppleholt's arms and legs flung off the lawn chair at angles even more absurd than the dog's. Thomas was nowhere in sight, and Carrie moaned out loud. It was just what she needed, to lose Thomas on top of everything else, and she clenched her fists and her teeth at Nuppleholt, who never kept his promises, but whom she was never allowed to backtalk. And for a moment, just for a moment, she would have accepted it, she would have said, okay Lord, let me have it, if I can only throw a rock at Nuppleholt's jaw and render it unsnuffrubbable for the rest of his life. But, instead, she shunted her rage into screaming for Thomas at the top of her lungs. Down the ditch a little ways from where the wreck had been, Thomas's groundhog-colored head reared out of the deep weeds. Nuppleholt, peeved at being awakened, raised up from his chair a few inches and slitted his eyes at her.

"What's the matter with you?" he asked. "You been acting real peculiar lately." Then he bugged the eyes wide open and stared like he could see straight into her stomach, and into her own brain flashed the image of a peanut-shaped and veined thing with an enormous mouth. She stalked off to the outhouse to deny him the pleasure of seeing her cry.

It was an old outhouse back along the creek, so long unused it no longer even stank, just had that dried-up musty smell old ones get. She peeled off her shorts and then her underpants. Even in the skinny slat of light falling through a broken board in the back, she could see plainly that the underwear was white. Unstained. Spotless.

"Fuck." She practiced the word, speaking it out loud to the shit-house walls. "Fuck." Her mother would wallop her in the back of the thighs with a wooden spoon if she heard, but Carrie figured she'd earned the right to speak it.

She drooped down onto the hole and started to sniffle. After a few minutes, she pulled her compact out of her pocket and studied her face, her chin scooping away so quick she had barely a chin at all, she saw, and her eyes pointing in at her nose under the careful turquoise shadow. Her makeup was a ruin, what with the sweat and the tears, and under it, crusty, she could see clear the white-capped pimples.

"Hoomid!" It was Thomas, rattling the door for attention. "It's hoomid!"

"Go away, Thomas," she muttered. She took a few more breaths of the outhouse funk, it not even occurring to her to pray anymore, then she fished a wad of Kleenex out of her other pocket and wiped all the wet off her face. Depositing the wad in the pit, she took a final deep inhale and exited regally from the privy into the little path leading to the bait stand. She scowled in the direction of Nuppleholt. She'd made a conscious decision to retain her dignity until the end of her shift.

Now pulling up to the stand was a van packed with bleached-looking kids who bubbled out of every crack before their father had the thing in park. Several immediately dove over the bank to the creek, the wilted father shouting after them to keep their shoes dry, while the youngest wandered straight into the highway and one almost as small got a hold of Nuppleholt's Grape Fanta can. "Too much sugar," Nuppleholt commented. He sat back to see what the child would do when it tasted the tobacco juice, but Carrie wrenched it away just as he got it to his lips. The father, with the kid he had retrieved from the road folded under his arm like a newspaper, wiped the sweat off his forehead by tucking it into his armpit. He asked Nuppleholt, "Who wrecked?"

"Reverend Metheny," Nuppleholt said, naming the Baptist minister.

Carrie watched the father's bland and wrung-out face stagger through shock and then confusion. She noticed that it ventured nowhere near disbelief. "Wah-h-h . . . Wahhh . . . " he fumbled. "I just saw the Reverend coming out of the Super Fresh!"

"Well," said Nuppleholt. "Guess he wasn't too badly boogered up, was he?"

At the far end of the turnaround, Thomas toiled over his First Aid kit. Carrie's suspicions began to rise. It would have been much more natural for him to have followed the kids to the creek. Then Archie started to take as much interest in Thomas's project as Thomas did, Thomas having to push his muzzle away with one hand while he worked with the other. The father was in the midst of a gory tale about a schoolbus wreck in Kentucky. As Carrie snuck up on Thomas, she saw that he had peeled the backs off a half dozen Band Aids to bandage a smallish object. When he finally spied her, he threw it into the shoebox and clapped on the lid.

"Thomas! What're you doing?"

Thomas wedged the box tightly between his elbow and his side, his lips set like cement.

"What you got there?" Knowing better than to reach for it, she squatted in front of him, watching him close and waiting him out. Within a few minutes, his arm relaxed, just a fraction. Carrie whipped out her hand and snatched the box.

She raced away as fast as she could move in her plastic sandals, Archie on her heels and Thomas right behind him, to the outhouse where she leapt through the door and slammed and latched it behind her. Thomas grabbed the handle, shaking it and bellowing, now the hyperactive kids, she heard, thrashing up over the bank to see what was happening, and Nuppleholt hollering that she knew better than to devil her uncle and trying to call off Archie by screaming his full name, Archmoore, to show he meant business. Carrie sat down over the hole and opened the box. The Band-Aid-swaddled object lay in the Ace band-age, and as she picked it up, a little clotting blood squeezed out onto her hands. She unbundled it. She was left with a scrap of something she couldn't identify.

She stood up on the seat to hold it directly in the sun through the broken board. Thomas had nearly jerked the latch out of the rotting wood by this time, the bleachy kids hammering on all four walls, Archie baying like he had something treed. Standing there straddling the hole with her legs splayed out, turning the bloody piece in the light, she felt something give a little between her thighs.

She shifted to make certain. There was an ooze, no doubt about it. Carrie felt she might float right out the roof.

Thank you, Jesus. She had started.

GETTING WOOD

It starts about five a.m. Chunks of wood hitting the back of the stove, the iron door slamming and catching. My father shuffles around, talking, not to anyone, and then he coughs. I wince. Down the road, somebody's rooster, somebody's dog, somebody starts their car for an early shift. My father feeds the fire.

Two hours later he's at my door. "Going up Four Square to get a load. Gotta get a jag on this morning. It'll be cold, cold tonight. Get up and help us if you want," the very tail of it just for manners because I don't live here anymore.

I step out the back door, take the morning like a fist in my chest. Seasons come sharp here, mid-November and already all the color stung out of the hills, those near etched with bare trees, gray behind, grading blue way back. I've seen plenty mountains since I left and I know these are different. Are not imposing or pretentious, don't make many people say, "Ahh." These mountains are.

My littlest brother's already waiting, hung from neck to knees in an oversized plaid jacket. He whispers in the ear of the bowlegged puppy he got for his twelfth birthday two weeks ago. "You gonna cut wood with us?" he asks me.

"Guess so," I say.

My father steps out, moving like mud. He surveys the sky and speaks to all three dogs. He pokes to the shed, sets the gas can and saw in the back of the pickup, pauses, says to my brother, "Tad, run get us a few apples." I can already see the end of my patience, but we're not going anywhere until my father wanders over to the woodpile, slips off his cap to ventilate his thinking, and studies the stack with great intent.

"Almanac says a long, long winter."

He tells me to drive so he can look out the window even though I can't see that there's anything to look at, bald brush and last year's leaves, brittle puddles in the dirt road. Because he'll only take what's already dead, when we reach a favorable spot he swings out of the truck, then plods around thumping trees with his walking stick, asking each out loud if it's ready to come down or not. I guess one sorry-looking pin oak agrees. My father remarks, "Gypsy moth got it." He fools with the saw, warns Tad and Tad's puppy away.

I hoist myself onto the tailgate, my back to my father, hands in my ears against the saw, and know that they do this every Saturday. Every Saturday. After my father works and Tad goes to school all week, they just do this, then spend Sunday morning at church, and go back to work and school on Monday. This is what they do at home. And what I don't know is why I keep coming back, feeling like I forgot something. Then leaving without it again.

Tad's already ricking up stovelengths, grunting, but not complaining. He's the youngest of seven and so skinny seems to me everything got used up before it was his turn to come. I help him. We trade places. One of us carries, the other in the truck bed stacks, balances. Soon it feels like we've been loading for a long time. Rote work like this always wears a rut down my mind until I feel it hit some nerve and all I want is it over. We heat up, strip off our coats. I bruise a knee, skin a couple fingers. It's not easy work for an eighty-pound boy, a middle-aged man, and a woman who lives out of state and warms the house by a dial, but all I can read of Tad is he's not thinking that, if he's thinking at all.

My father decides we've earned a break. We sit side by side on a decaying log, all three of us with saw still in our ears. He quarters an apple, Tad talks about his math class the day before, the puppy worries us for a hunk of apple he doesn't know what to do with when he gets it. Then my father stops and says, "Listen. Just listen." Tad grins at me out of the side of his face while his puppy walks himself into a circle to rest, his muzzle splayed across Tad's boot. And I try, but my head's too loud.

As I walk away, I'm ashamed each time my foot shatters leaves, then ashamed about being ashamed. At last, I'm safe behind the truck where I can think without their listening getting in my way. I gaze back at my youngest brother, hunkered over the log like a grasshopper. I wonder how he can make his mind stay still. How he can just sit there and listen.

I've only been here seven days, but it seems like a couple months. Time's like that here, dammed up someplace nobody sees. It was worse when I lived here, heavy and close, too much time all the time, my mind turning over and over and over, wading those thick damp summers sticking to my sheets and talking to myself, *gonna get out of here, got to get out of here, when I get out of here. . . .* And again, last night, after six full days, I felt myself strain. Strain, I told myself in those summers, to make *any*thing happen, just so it was *some*thing.

Now I know it's for anything just so it's something else.

Yesterday I saw my oldest friend. She and her husband eat hamburger casserole for supper, put in a garden every year, take their children to Sunday School, never miss the county fair parade. We all—her, me, the kids—sat down on their new living-room sofa and had Pepsi in plastic cups, her saying, "Remember when we . . ." and "Remember when we . . ." When we were sixteen years old and drank wide-mouthed Mickies, fumbled with boys in the rank orchard grass. Denim rubbing across our fronts, the odor of fermenting apples. When it was both hot and cold enough to see breath in the dark, and past shoulders, branches put scratches in the sky.

When some of us got away with it, and some of us didn't.

Then that was done, and she talked in the now, told how this one was writing her name, just a little backwards, and how that one dreamed bad and slipped in between them at night, and I knew that although neither one of us was happy, she'd learned not to ask her disappointment as many questions.

As she changed the diaper on her latest, he arched his back and struck air with his fists, wound up his face to cry.

"Shh," she murmured. "Be still now."

My father and Tad have started back to work and I watch him grind away at mental intervals he's eyed out up and down the log. Tad tramps back and forth through a little rut he's worn in the leaves, arms piled to right below his eyes, puppy in front of and behind his legs. When the bed won't take any more, my father cases the saw and we lean against the fender. He buries his nose in an orange handkerchief. "Well, you going back tomorrow?"

"Guess so," I say.

He takes the wheel and heads back down, humming something in snatches like he's playing it in his head and doesn't notice the out-loud part. Tad pivots on his knees and squats backwards to keep an eye on the load. I'm nearest the window and try to focus as the brush sweeps by. I see myself drive out of here tomorrow without it again. I need to say or do something now, but my thoughts are so wadded I can't get hold of a single word to begin. My mind turns over and over, muddying itself until the only clear part is where the something else should be in the very middle Finally, my confusion is so loud I think they must hear it.

But they don't.

When we pull up to the house, Tad scrambles over me and races inside for his lunch, his puppy after him. My father flows out of the cab on the other side and I follow.

"Dad," I start, but it's too big in me to take out.

He looks over his shoulder, slow, and studies me.

"Give me a hand with this wood," he says.

REDNECK BOYS

Richard has gone on and died, she thinks when she hears the knuckle on the door. Took two weeks after the accident, he was strong. The other three dead at the scene. She glances at the digital clock on top of Richard's New Testament, then she covers her face with her hands. The yellow stink of the hospital still hangs in her hair. It's 3:07 a.m., and Richard has gone on and died.

She pulls on yesterday's jeans and feels her way through the hall, not ready yet for a light in her eyes. Cusses when she hits barefoot the matchbox cars her son's left lying around. She's so certain it's her brother, who was made messenger back towards the beginning of this mess, she doesn't even pull back the curtain to see. She stops behind the door to steady her breath, which is coming quick and thin even though she's expected the news for days. But when she unbolts the door, it is a boy, a man, she hasn't seen in a few years.

He blows steam in the porchlight, straddling the floor frame Richard never had time to finish. Coatless, his arms pork-colored in the cold. He has forced himself into corduroy pants he's outgrown and wears a pair of workboots so mudcaked they've doubled in size. He grins. She knew him some time ago. And he grins at her, his face gone swollen, then loose under the chin, the way boys get around here.

"Cam," is what he says.

She draws back to let Splint pass. He unlaces the muddy boots and leaves them on the ground under the porch frame. The surprise she might have felt if he'd shown up before Richard's wreck—and she's not sure she would have felt surprise then—has been wrung out of her by the two-week vigil. Splint walks to the sofa where he wraps himself in an afghan and chafes his upper arms with his palms. He swipes at the runny nose with his shoulder. Cam remembers what she's wearing—just a long-john shirt of Richard's over the jeans, no bra—and for a moment, her face heats with self-consciousness. Then the heat leaves her face for other places in her body. Angry at herself, Cam wills the heat away.

"Where's your boy?" Splint asks. Then, "I heard about Richard."

"Down to Mom's," Cam answers.

"You're up on this mountain without even a dog at night?"

Splint squats in front of the woodstove, still shawled in the afghan that doesn't quite fall to his waist. Cam watches the soft lobs between the waistband of the cordu-roys and the hem of the hiked-up T-shirt. Burrs snagged in his pantscuffs. Cam wonders what he's done now to end up coatless in the middle of a freezing night. Then she doesn't wonder. She crouches on the edge of the sofa be-hind him, her chest clenched, and she waits for what he'll do next.

What he does is open the stove door and huddle up to it closer, giving Cam a better look at his soft back. Hound-built he was as a boy, a little bowlegged and warped along the spine, the new muscles riding long and taut and rangy right under the skin. Freckle-ticked shoulders. She recalls trailing him one August afternoon up a creekbed where he'd stashed a six-pack of Old Milwaukee in sycamore roots. He'd outgrown that shirt, too, a tank top, and she had watched it ride up, watched the tight small of his back. The muscles coming so soon, too early, on those boys.

"Why don't you poke up the fire for me?" Splint startles her. She starts to move, then pauses, asks herself who she's answering to and why. But she's been raised to obedience. She leans forward and picks up a split chunk on the hearth. Its raw insides tear the skin on her palm, even though it is a hard hand that has handled many stovelogs. She shoves the log in the embers, kneels, and blows until the coals flare up. Then, as she reaches to shut the door, Splint's own hand snakes out of the afghan and grabs her arm. Cam goes icy in the roots of her hair. She yanks away, harder than she needs to. The stove door stays open, the pipe drawing hard and loud. A sizzle and whupping in the flue.

"It's too bad about Richard," Splint says. "He was always a good boy."

Cam can't tell if he's mocking her.

"And a hard worker, huh?"

This is funeral talk, and Cam doesn't answer.

"You never were a big talker," Splint says. "Guess you don't got any cigarettes around here?"

He pulls a big splinter from the stove to light the Virginia Slim she gives him. Cam knows he knows Richard is just like the others. Went down off the mountain at five a.m. to meet his ride, traveled two hours to build northern Virginia condominiums all day, traveled the hundred miles back to a six-room house he was putting together on weekends and didn't finish before the wreck. Celotex walls and the floors unsanded. Yeah, Richard was a hard worker, just like all the other boys. Only Splint wouldn't work hard, and Splint ended up in jail.

"I still think about you," he says. He'd been staring into the stove, but now he cocks his head sidewise to look at Cam, kneeling a little behind him. She has her bare feet drawn up under her, and not just for warmth. To be all of a piece like that, pulled together, makes her feel safe from herself. Her eyes drift to his hands in the firelight there, them hanging loose in his lap. It occurs to her she has never seen them so clean although the heat draws an odor from his body, the odor of ground in the woods. But the hands— no grease in the knuckle creases or in the prints, the nails clear and unbroken. Back when she knew him, the hands were all the time dirty. He spent half his time with his head in an engine, the other half under the chassis. Frittered his cash away on parts and auto wrecker junk, and when it still wouldn't run, he'd steal. What've you been into now, buddy? Cam thinks. Splint pulls up the tail of his shirt to stob his running nose.

The last time she and Splint ran, they were seniors in high school. Splint told her to meet him a ways down her road so her parents wouldn't see, and he showed up in a brand-new Camaro, she recognized the car. Sixteenth-birthday present to some lawyer's kid at school, but Splint was playing his own music. Lynryd Skynyrd. Cam got drunk before they hit the paved road, grain alcohol and orange pop, the music thrushing through her stomach and legs, while Splint cussed the car for handling like a piece of shit. She cranked down her window, stuck her head in the wind. Wind, leaves, hills, but no sky. Sky too far overhead to see from a car. Just ground, pounding by on either side. It was spring, and by that time, they knew about the college, the scholarship.

They eventually reached Frawl's Flat, the second

straightest piece of road in the county, and they started seeing how fast the Camaro would go. Stupid-drunk like they
were, the state police snuck up on them easy. Splint
squealed off down the highway, and even though the car
was a piece of shit, they might have outrun the cops, or,
more likely, could have ditched the car and both run off in
the woods. But Splint did something else.

He swerved back a narrow, heavy-wooded road,
braked, and screamed at Cam to get out, shoving at her
shoulder as he yelled. And Cam did. She tumbled out, the
car down to maybe fifteen miles an hour by then, landed
on her hip in the ditch, then scrambled up the shale bank
into the scrub oak and sumac. The staties were so close
they caught Splint where she could watch. Crouched in the
brush, cold sober, she saw the three of them moving in and
out the headlights and taillights. He'd just turned eighteen,
and they put him in jail for a while that time. They didn't
know to look for Cam.

"Oh, you were bright," Splint is saying, and she winces
at how the gravel has come in his craw. Tobacco voice.
"Bright. All that running around you did and they still
gave you a scholarship."

Cam doesn't answer back. Splint knows there was one
person in their class as bright as Cam, and that was Splint.
She knows Splint knows she got a boy instead of a college
degree. She realizes she's unnumbed enough to need a
drink, and she heads to the kitchen to fetch one. Aware of
what Splint will want, she starts to open the refrigerator,
then stops. On the door, her boy's drawings, motorcycles
and eighteen-wheelers. Instead, she pulls a bottle of Jim
Beam and two jelly glasses from the crates they are using
until they have money for cabinets. The whiskey she and
Richard shared, but the beer in the refrigerator belongs to
just Richard.

She even called Splint once or twice during the year she spent at the university in gray Morgantown. Then she left the state and saw a little of the world, ha. Waited tables in Daytona for eight months before she met a boy named Eric, and they went west, that was for six. What she remembers best—or worst—at any rate, what she remembers clearest—is the way this Eric talked. In six months, she never could get used to it. Hardened every consonant, choked up every vowel. Such an awkward, a cramped way to work your words out your mouth. It got to where she couldn't stand to hear him say her name, how he'd clip it off, one syllable. Cam. Like he had no idea about the all of her. Back home, they speak it full. They say it Ca-yum. Back here.

Splint drains his glass, shivers his head and shoulders, stretches. The afghan drops to the floor. He swaggers over to Richard's gun cabinet, and Cam sees how he carries himself like a middle-aged man. Still small in his hips, he is, but big across the belly, and him no more than thirty. Although her eyes stay on Splint, her mind sees her own body at the same time. She knows she's gone in the other direction, a rare way to go around here. Cam knows she's worn rutted and flat. Splint strokes the rifle stocks along their grains, draws one out and pretends to sight it down the hall. It is Richard's, and Cam feels an urge to lift it from Splint's hands. Between his third and fourth fingers, the cigarette smolders, there under the finger playing the trigger. "Pow," Splint says.

She'd known she'd never stay with Eric, but Richard was just something that happened when she came home for Christmas. Fifteen minutes in Richard's dad's pickup behind the Moose, the windows fogged, and then Richard sat up with his jeans around his ankles and printed their names in the steam. Like a twelve-year-old girl, Cam thought at the time. Some little twelve-year-old girl. No, she never felt for Richard. What she felt for Splint. She was so fresh back home she was still homesick and she just wanted to hear them talk, talk to her, it could have been any boy who talked that way. She ran into Richard that night. But Richard was a good boy and a hard worker, everybody said so. She could have done way worse; her mom made sure to remind her of this often. After a while, she wrote Eric in Phoenix. (Seventy-five, eighty miles an hour across that flat Oklahoma, Texas, New Mexico. Highways like grooves, and the land. She fixed that land, she remade it every night. She dreamed it green where it was brown, rumpled it where flat.) He wrote back once. Told her he always knew she'd end up with some redneck boy.

The second time she and Splint ran, they were thirteen. They met at the end of her road right around dawn, the hills smoking fog twists and a damp raw in the air. They flagged the Greyhound when it came, the Greyhound would pick you up anywhere back then, but although they'd had their sights set on North Carolina, the money Splint thieved off his older sister got them no farther than middle-of-nowhere Gormania. When the driver realized they'd ridden past how far they could pay, he threw them off at a mountaintop truck stop and told the cook to call the sheriff.

The deputy who showed up had only one ear. He phoned their parents with the receiver flat against the ear-hole. It was Cam gave him the numbers, and Splint wouldn't speak to her for four weeks after. She remembers Splint all tough over his black coffee in that drafty restaurant, pretending Cam wasn't there. The waitress locking up the cigarette machine. The deputy told her how his ear got shot off stalking deer poachers, but after he left, the cook said his wife did it with sewing scissors. When Splint's dad appeared, three hours later, he, too, pretended Cam wasn't there. He jerked Splint to his feet and dragged him out behind the building while Cam slunk along the wall to watch. Splint slouched between the Stroehmann bread racks and raw kitchen slop. The scraggly garbage birds in a panic. But his father just looked at him and shook his head, then cussed him without imagination. The same two words, over and over, his voice flat as an idling motor. In the constant wind across the mountaintop, his father's coveralls flapped against his legs, making them look skinnier than they were. Finally he threw a milk crate at Splint. Splint caught it.

"I still think about you," Splint is saying again. He has put away the rifle and settles on the sofa, leaving her room which she doesn't take. He's trying to start something, but this time, she tells herself, she won't follow.

Richard always called it love. Ten years of late suppers and, even on weekends, him asleep in front of the TV by eight p.m. Two hours later, he'd wake and they'd shift to the bed, the brief bucking there. Afterwards, he'd sleep again, as sudden and as deep as if he'd been cold-cocked. Richard was a good boy and a hard worker. And now he's waited for two weeks, in his patient, plodding way, to be killed in a car wreck. That week's driver asleep at the wheel ten miles short of home after a day of drywalling.

Cam feels as tired as if she'd been awake for all her thirty years.

The first time she and Splint had run, they were twelve years old, at 4-H camp. The camp lay five miles back a dirt road where they hauled kids in schoolbuses until the mountains opened into a sudden clearing along the river. Like a secret place. The county had turned 1950s chicken coops into bunkhouses and jammed them mattress to mattress with castoff iron beds, and Cam slept uneasy there under the screenless windows, the barnboard flaps propped open for the little air. She had seen Splint at school, but this was the first time she noticed. And as she watched from a distance, she heard what was live in him like a dog might hear it. What was live in him, she heard a high-pitched whine. The beds in the coop were packed so close together she could feel on her cheeks the nightbreath of the girls on either side. And the whine a hot line from her almost-breasts to her navel.

On the last evening, they had a Sadie Hawkins shotgun wedding, where the girls were supposed to catch the boys. The counselors lined them up, the boys with a fifty-foot headstart, then blew a whistle and turned them loose. Cam aimed at Splint. Splint knew she was after him, and he headed towards the river, where they were forbidden to go. All around Cam, big girls seized little squealy boys, older boys faked half-hearted escapes. Splint fled, but at twelve, Cam was his size, and as fast, and as strong. She saw him disappear in the treeline along the river, then she was dodging through trees herself, and she caught up with him on the rock bar there. Panting, but not yet spent, she reached out to grab him, but she scared, then just touched at him like playing tag. Splint was trotting backwards, bent in at the waist, dodging and laughing. They heard others following them to the river, heard them hollering through the trees. "Pretend you ain't caught me yet," Splint said.

He wheeled and sloshed into the river, high stepping until the water hit his hips, then he dropped on his stomach and struck out swimming. Cam, just as strong, as swift, right behind.

The far side had no shore to it, just an eroded mud bank. They hauled themselves up the exposed maple roots, and then they were in woods, they were hidden, alone. Cam was twelve years old, she thought she knew what to do. Splint grappled her back, too much teeth in the kiss, his hands in unlikely places. They rubbed at each other through their soaked clothes, serious and quick, and the threat of the others swimming the river pushed them faster.

Cam was finding her way, so absorbed it was like being asleep, when she realized Splint wasn't doing anything back. He rolled away from her into the weeds and sat up with his face between his knees, his thin back to her. Too naive to feel hurt, Cam crawled closer. She heard a strange little animal noise that made her want to pet. Finally, she understood Splint was crying.

Something taps her feet folded under her. Splint has rolled his jelly glass across the floor.

"Girl, if you don't talk to me, I'm going to do something drastic."

Cam looks at him. "What are you doing up here in the middle of the night without a coat?"

Splint laughs, soft. "Got into it with a girl driving home. She threw me out of her car." He rises off the sofa, leans down to open the stove door, and strips away his T-shirt. He stands fat in front of the fire, soaking heat in his skin.

Cam's all the time finding her own boy sketching pickup trucks and stock cars on notebook paper, oh, he is careful, detailed and neat. Until the very end. Then something breaks in him, unstops, and he turns violent and free. He gouges deep black lines behind the vehicles to show how fast they can go. When he was littler, and they still lived in Richard's parents' basement, he'd ride the back of the couch like a motorcycle, forcing air through his lips for the throttle. That he is not Richard's, she is almost sure, but he seems not Eric's either. Seems mothered and fathered by her and the place. She stands next to Splint now, following his stare in the fire. Without looking at her, Splint lifts her hand and presses it against his naked side.

"I'm not having sex with you," Cam says.

"That's not how come I'm here," says Splint.

He drops her hand and walks to the closet behind the front door. He pulls out a quilted flannel shirt of Richard's and buttons it on. Shoving aside the blaze-orange hunting jacket and coats that belong to Cam, he finally reaches the end of the rack and mutters.

"He's got his good one back in the bedroom," Cam says.

She finds the big Sunday coat. Splint takes it. Cam doesn't think about offering him a ride until after he's gone.

He got mad about the crying, screwed his fists in his eyes and muddied his face. Cam mumbled it didn't matter. By that time, counselors were yelling at them from across the water, how much trouble they were in if they didn't come right back. Cam stood up and Splint followed. They crept out of the trees and climbed down the bank without looking at the grownups. They waded out to thigh-deep and started paddling.

They pulled that water slow, kicked sloppy. They were putting off their punishment. Cam remembers the water still springtime cold a foot under the surface, this was June. The eyeball green of the river, and how you could see current only in the little bubble clusters gliding down its top. She swam a little behind Splint, her head about parallel with his stomach, and when she remembers back, she understands how young he was. Twelve, same as her, yes, but a boy-twelve, and she thinks of her own son and feels sad and shameful for how she did Splint.

Because she was so close to him as they swam, and because she couldn't help but look at him, and because the way they glided along cut the water clean—no foam to speak off, no wave—Cam saw clearly what happened next.

She saw Splint break his stroke to reach out and toss aside a floating stick. His legs frogged behind him. This was about the solstice, it was still very light, she could see. He reached out, not looking too closely, not paying attention. He was just moving a thing in his way. But when Splint grabbed hold the branch, Cam saw it liven in his fist and change shapes. She saw it spill water, jerk curvey in his hand. She saw it uncurl itself upright over Splint's head.

And was it a snake before he grabbed hold, or after he did? Cam used to wonder before she grew up. Now she only wonders why neither of them screamed.

CROW SEASON

Seems I dreamed it several times before. Me wandering a hollow, branching into hollow, branching into hollow. Dream my shoulders passing through that up and down land, and the dead leaves, snakeskin-dry and slippery. Ground up over my head (the way you're in land over your head). And the sudden reek of dead animal, but you can't see the carcass except for the crows. Hollow, branching into hollow, branching into hollow. Until it all closes up in a draw, and there are no more hollows.

*   *   *

I heard it in Ranson the morning after. What my youngest uncle's youngest boy had done. When I got off work, I ate a can of chili and sat on my porch, deciding. Then I drove down to the homeplace to see if I could help.

*   *   *

I call out from the back door, then let myself into a kitchen odored of tuna cans and old smoke. Soiled dishes stacked.

My uncle eats from a McDonald's bag, and he is odored, too, unbathed, unshaved. He eats from the bag furtive, as though it is a sin.

—Ravelle never could control that boy.

He speaks of his second wife, the boy's mother, who has left him now. I just nod, like I tend to do.

—I knew he'd done some looting up in there. I found a few bottles. But I didn't know he was selling it to other kids.

I nod again. Through the window behind my uncle, everything's coming up thistle and chicory and Queen Anne's lace, weeds that thrive on a drought. No difference between yard and pasture, no difference between pasture and field. Under a dead apple tree, a big dog feeds from a loose refrigerator drawer. I'm thinking. Although I'm not sure, I figure Vincent'll be in one of two places. Not too many hiding places back in the mountain with any water to speak of in this kind of dry.

—I was never moved to do much about it.

I look from the window back to his face.

—The looting, I mean. Hell, far as I'm concerned, underneath up there will always be ours.

—Underneath Joby Knob, I say.

—Hell, yeah, Joby Knob. He works a piece of gristle out of his teeth. How was I supposed to know how hard those people are? He shakes his head. People hard enough to poison liquor to teach a child thief a lesson.

*　*　*

I pick the Heplinger Place first, and I choose to walk. And not only because the truck motor will give Vincent warning and make him run. The deer paths in the hollows have been beaten big as cattle crossings, with the size of the herds now and the terrible drought. I place my feet careful, watching for every stick to move. *Snakes'll come out of the high places in dries like this,* I hear my father. The drought has shrunk all the creeks into a few holes, and the earth around these holes, punched solid with deer tracks.

Most of this land would have been my inheritance, and I grew up hunting it, cutting wood off it, running it. I know it better than anyone still living, including the man who owns it now. Never have I seen it so tired, with the deer paths wide as cattle runs up and down the hollow sides, and acornless ground. And the deer themselves, gaunt and puny and sorrowed. Quivering under their flies.

* * *

From where I sat in the kitchen, I could see behind the stove a ripped sleeping bag where the dog must stay. Unbaited mousetraps scattered in corners. My father and uncles grew up in this house, their father and grandfather, too. I'd been told there were rooms upstairs now where you could see sky. But I hadn't climbed to the second story in twenty years.

—You know they say the Haslacker boy may or may not live. The one he sold the bottle to.

I nodded.

—Vincent has Knob inside him. It's not a matter of who holds the paper. You know that.

The oven door was open to where I could see burnt cheese all over its bottom. Although my uncle sacrificed the house upkeep to save the land, he had to sell off anyway, including Joby Knob.

—Well, either you know better than any of us it's not a matter of who holds the paper. Or you don't know it at all.

I looked at the man across the table. There was a darkness in my uncle. I used not to fear him when I was
younger, but the darkness had come in him, and I feared
him now. The anger hardening some place in his body.
Where eventually it would crack loose and bolt to his
brain.

*   *   *

I angle to the right, a hollow branching off the Shingle
Hollow, a shortcut to the Heplinger Place. A leaf layer
sprouts feet, takes on substance, weight. A fawn flushing.
This was a road at one time, but I can only see road if I un-
focus my eyes.

The Heplinger Place is a little bigger than the Further
House, the other spot Vincent might be. The last people to
live here were bark strippers with two daughters, one crippled by a gun, but they all four died of typhoid not long
after the turn of the century. At least that's what my father
always said. But he was known to make things up. I scout
around the rubble of house and barn, find a litter of shotgun shells, a Snickers wrapper from last fall. And then the
old stuff, metal and stone. A harness buckle. A barrel
stave. No sign Vincent has been through.

Just as I'm about to leave, I hear behind me a peculiar
misplaced sound. Wavery, and I stop to listen harder. A cat
noise, I'm thinking, but crossed with something wild. I
turn slowly in a circle, the dry sky turning overhead, and I
understand it comes from the old bad well. I listen. A crow
throats from a hickory tree. Typhoid, I remember, and all
of them dead, and I know inside me a wrongness and grief
out of all proportion to common sense.

I can't see where the well was, buried in dead leaves,
but I remember stumbling over it several times in the past.

I listen. The well mewls again. A hot dry wind rattles through, a wind doesn't belong here. *A Western wind, I call it.* I hear my father say this so clear I wonder for a second if he's in that well, too. I trace the mewling to the rotty cover. I squat over it, clear away the leaves. Then I break off a soft board and peer inside.

The moment the sun falls through, two eyes flash a flat green. Then they go out. I stare harder, but the creature's shrunk from the light. It does not sound again.

Something curls inside me. The dry has drawn it into the well, and there it starves and won't ever get out. And me the last thing to see it, and I can't even tell what it is.

* * *

Not many weeks ago, I drove up on Joby Knob myself, ignoring the "Posted." It is a foreign place to me now. The developers renamed it Misty Mountain Estates, acre clearings of new houses built to look old. Each lot is armored with a security system and warning signs, and that Vincent even managed to break into one of these places I can't help but admire. A different kind of hunting. Rows of second homes on a clear-cut ridge, up here where no old-timer would ever build. *Those old-timers built in the bottoms and the hollows* (again, my father), *out of the wind and near water.* As I rode along the smooth-graded gravel road, I squinted to find the good crossing place, where I'd shot a big-bodied eight-point when I was seventeen or so. But near as I could tell, the crossing ran straight through a kit log cabin. And the feel of moving among all those new vacation houses, yet not a soul around. The houses creating an expectation of presence, then their emptiness sucking that expectation inside out. So much emptier on Joby Knob now than when it was just trees.

Back before, we'd drive to the power cut to see off. Now you can see off anywhere, but I went to the power cut that day. I leaned against the grill of my truck and looked up and down the valley, several miles in both directions. The drought-stricken trees turning already, even though it was July.

The darkness in my father, too, would wax and wane. He'd have me convinced he'd finally gone pure mean, then he'd do me something kind. He never let me find my footing there. But I learned. I learned I'd never care about anything so much the loss of it would turn me dark.

I climbed into the bed of my truck where I could get a better view and looked out over the cab. The way the land lays in here looks more like a human body than any land I've ever seen, pictures or real. And I often wonder if that's the reason for the hold it has on us.

*   *   *

As I pass back through the Deep Hollow to where I'll pick up the jeep track to the Further House, I hear a truck motor. I stop and wait. It is several minutes, and the flies find me good, before I see my uncle's truck. He leans his head and his arm through the window.

—I got news you can give him that might flush him out.

*   *   *

The night before, he'd spoken of my father. Though not directly. He'd talked of the strokes, that family vulnerability: his mother, his brother, his father, mine. He spoke not for the loss of them, I knew, but out of fear for himself. Fear of his own blood drying inside him. Making a seed.

116

He spoke like a drunk man, and I wish that was so. But didn't none of them drink. They could crazy themselves on air. I watched my uncle scratch the insides of his arms, and I wondered if he felt the clotting under his skin.

* * *

As I climb the jeep track towards the Further House, I wonder from which house Vincent stole the liquor. I picture Joby Knob in my head. One place has an observatory, of all things, another a swimming pool. And one a burglar alarm so sensitive it goes off every time it thunderstorms and I can hear it all the way down to my house. Then I try to imagine the weekenders who did it. I imagine. To poison your own liquor to catch the boy who stole from you.

I finally come up over the last ridge and creep out on a shale point where I can spy down into the flat. I right away see the boy's tarp rigged in a corner of the stone foundation. I let a little shale spill off the bank under my boots to make him look. His face upturns, sooty, smoky. Peering up at me. Him on his haunches and hands like a dog.

"Vincent. Vincent Keadle," I call. "Come on out of there."

Then I can't see him, but I hear him break away through the brush and scramble up the far bank, his tennis shoes slipping in the barrens. Him, again, I know, on his haunches and hands.

"Vincent," I call after him. "They say the boy is going to live."

* * *

Let me tell you this. I was a few years older than Vincent Keadle when we lost all but the thirty acres down around

117

the house. My father left with his hunting rifle, and this was late spring, the season for nothing. He took the truck, so I had to walk, but he abandoned it a half mile up the Deep Hollow, and the ground was wet, him easy to track. Hollow branching into hollow, and me mounting up, hollow, into draw, into crease, until I'd top a ridge, catch my breath, slide to the bottom and start again. And, yes, I was thinking, what if he shoots me. But I tell myself (I tell myself) I worried more for him.

When I got close enough to glimpse his red coat, I trailed at a distance until he staggered to a stop. Then I snuck over the leaves, them muted with the wet, and hid in the catface of a fire-scarred oak. There I watched him load it, and I knew it was my place to dart out and wrestle it away. But I did not. I squatted in that catface, pressed so tight against the bark it left scratches in my cheek. Saw my father raise the gun, snug the stock against his shoulder, pause and look around.

Then I watched him fire in the ground. Empty and empty it into lost ground.

* * *

—Sometimes it's hard to look at you, boy. My uncle balled up his McDonald's bag and pitched it to the end of the table with the other trash, mostly unopened mail. I studied the empty blood-thinner bottles rowed up in the sill.

—I used to think you were weak, he told me. But anymore. Anymore I wonder if you're the only one of all you kids was born with any sense.

He leaned in closer to me. Gouged, his eyes looked, in that beginning-to-get-dark.

—Probably not, he said.

*   *   *

I grew up in it. Forever, the mutter and drone. The anxiety, the obsession, the fear, the fights: the farm, the money, the family, the past.

Years ago, I made my decision. I sold off my inheritance except an acre.

*   *   *

By the time I get all the way back to the paved road, Vincent sits with his head bowed in his father's truck. I catch my uncle's eye in his side mirror. He nods at me, then looks away, but he doesn't look at Vincent either. I walk a quarter mile of asphalt to where I left my own truck, climb in, and drive the last mile home.

I keep no mirrors in my place. I tell what I look like in others' faces, me make-them-gasp identical. I know that I've grown into a ghost. Carrying in my face, in how my body's hung together, in how I speak and move, the man who died and made me take over the looks of him. But I'm used to my outsides. What scares me is if it's printed on my insides, too.

I wait here on my single acre. I hoe my garden. I water the trees.

CASH CROP: 1897

＝

The sun makes a short trip in the short sky over their place. Buries its head in the mountain, tunnels all night under that hill, their hollow, two more ridges. Comes back up out of the earth. And Lil knows that night trip is not an easy one. She knows how hard that sun travels, boring the mountains. A long way under rough ground.

Usually she pulls with her face to the side where she can watch the muscles rise out of her dress. The flats of her hands blister, bust, leak pus on the harness. She tries to follow the pictures in the road under her feet, but dragging the cart makes that a hard thing to do. On the best days, she can see spirits flapping out of the shapes of the ruts, the braids of serpents in how the runoff does the shale, and once in a while a rock will carry a real picture, seashells mostly (she can see seashells in Lucy's books), and how seashells got up in these hills she does not know, but it is a wondrous thing. Used to be she imagined God sprinkling them down for her people to know a tiny miracle. Anymore she thinks it's hard to tell. Then if they hit a bad steep and she has to pull her hardest, she cannot see at all.

The sun stays much longer in the bottom, Lucy says. She knows because before her accident she spent many whole days working down there for the Keadles (it is Keadle gave her the books). Even though Lil's been in the bottom lots of times, it has never been from sunrise to sunset, but Lucy knows, and she's told her. Lucy grabs the cart wheels and shoves them forward with her hands. All of her parts that don't work anymore she has folded in a heap underneath her skirt. The gun rides beside the heap. It is rabbits she's after today even though she shouldn't be, them having their little ones now. But they'll pay cash for rabbits at the Club no matter what season it is, and not often do Mom and Pap tell Lucy no anymore.

Because it's rabbits she wants, Lil has to haul her over to the Jones place. And since Pap traded their rabbit dog for the cart last winter, it's Lil has to flush them. Road roughens to a bad track after they take the fork up towards that little flat where the Jones had lived and already moved off several years before Lil or even Lucy was born. Left a cutover place the sun can get to to raise the brush, the briers and stuff. What rabbits need to live in. Right before the woods break out into the clearing, she anchors the wagon with Lucy in it by jamming rocks behind the wheels. Then she circles round, keeping to the trees, a wide, wide circle that brings her out behind the old house. She looks at that house, quivering there in a last lean, and the berry bushes all over everything, softening it. She stands there thinking of Rosie, their old rabbit dog, and she wonders what the dog could scent from here. What the rabbit smells talked to her. Lucy waves the gun in the air to hurry her up.

Hooting and swatting with a stick, she rushes a long likely bundle of briers. Cottontails squirt out like water wrung from a wet towel, most of them just little fellows, scrambling the old yard between the house and Lucy. Lucy still has her good shoulder, her good finger, her very good eye. She drops two fat ones out of that bunch, and after Lil pushes her on over to the old fruit trees, she gets one more. Lil gathers the bunnies in a sack (the heaviness a dead thing will make something she will never get used to) and tucks the sack into the cart bed with Lucy's legs. When she harnesses back up, she feels her own legs. The muscles waiting under the skin and the motion waiting in the muscles. She reaches down to squeeze the rip a locust thorn left in her leg, and she forces blood from it. There sits beautiful Lucy, tall and half able out of the cart. She rides the brake back down the hill while Lil trots close behind where she can steady the cart if it tips in a rut. And all around them, the little green things trying to push up from under the dead leaves. It is the season for that.

*   *   *

She is younger, and dumber, and uglier than Lucy, but every last part of her moves. While Lucy holes up in the back of the house, drawing the comfort from her magazines (learning to want, Mom says, back in there learning to want), Lil sneaks out to the shed, the dark with the Bible window in it, and then it must all be done in order. First she squats with her back against old Bob's stall, in the old Bob smell with old Bob gone (Pap having sold him off last fall to pay town doctor bills, sold off all but his good smell, and his manure, dried now into shallow cakes, and, of course, his tack), then she stretches out flat in the clean dirt. Kind of dirt stays inside and never mixes with rain, and next she pulls her dress up over her waist. She raises her legs off the ground at her hips so when she rolls all the muscles she can see them move from her thighs to her feet, study those muscles moving under skin like a cloud shadow passing windy trees, and after she's done with that, she tends to the bones. She crooks, then she opens up, every joint she can find, flutters the little bird bones in her feet, explores all the ways of the ankle. Then she fingers the blood pressing full through the veins. Feels for the current of it. It was from old Bob's tack Pap fashioned the harness for Lucy's cart, Pap working hard over it during the winter, him not good at that kind of thing. He did the best that he could.

After she finishes moving and finishes it proper, she gazes up at the Bible window that makes seen what is behind the air (it is just dust, motes, Lucy says, there is nothing to see behind the air), the behind the air taking shape in loose-linked sparkles like it seems to Lil the Holy Ghost looks. And she lies there holding everything still. But these days the feel of it (the something warm with light in it) comes late and leaves early.

And then although that's supposed to be the end, she does something else. She sees herself turning on her belly like a snake. She limpens all her parts below her waist. She raises up on her knuckles, and makes to slip along like Lucy does. But even after all these months of dragging the cart, she is not strong enough. At least not strong enough in that way.

* * *

It is worst in the night. Not so much because of the dark, but because she is tiredest. Cart-worn, her muscles tailing off puny and yarned, and what is Lil, she knows, leaves with the muscles. Leaving like water spilled in the sun, Lil drying into the dark, and she balls her eyes white to make herself stay. Then her leg brushes Lucy's across the bed, and panicked, she jerks it away.

Lucy does not notice. She is whispering and muttering over the caves.

Never said a word about them before she got shot, but now she cannot leave them alone. How thirty years ago two black brothers knived to death a traveling faith healer who'd let the one man's boy die and hauled his body up the top of Lockenjer Mountain. It was Shell Red told her about them, the black woman with the strange milky splash on her neck, Lucy and Shell wiping dishes in Keadle's kitchen and Shell telling how they used a little terrier dog to open the cave mouth and then hid the body way back in a tunnel. *But they didn't take his money.*

Lil listens to Mom and Pap's snoring.

It's a terrible steep up the side of Lockenjer, she finally says.

Didn't take his money, Lucy says. Knew better'n that. That's not why they kilt him. Way we'll go is start right behind the Riley's place, in the creekbed there, Shell said, then you climb a beeline up the side of Lockenjer. Come out three ridges off of High Knob. One, two, three. If you come out right, you'll see rocks stuck up in the trees where somebody's marked the going-over place. Drop down just a little to a ledge, and under that ledge are what they call the warming dens. Holes in the rock pile where warm air comes up out of the ground, even in winter, now won't that be something to see?

Lil tries to make a belief for the caves come in her. She tries to do so gladly (*but for the grace of God goes you,* says Mom, *but for,* and the guilt that goes with the grace Lil got has made her do much harder things). But even if she can call up a little faith, it's still a faith too feeble to make that hard haul worth it. At least not in the night when she's dribbling away.

It's a terrible steep up the side of Lockenjer, she says.

Think how strong you are, Lil. You can get us up there.

Lil ponders that.

Mom and Pap been running these woods since they could walk, and they've never said nothing about any caves.

It's a nigger cave. What do Mom and Pap know about niggers?

Niggers, no. But caves they would know.

Didn't take his money, Lucy says. Knew better 'n that . . .

Lil saw Shell, just once. Her standing in the kitchen yard at Keadle's, she remembers it, looking up past the stoop. It was not long ago, she was probably twelve then, but already bigger than Lucy although Lucy's three years older. Sun coming down in a butter light, wet, it has less underground it must travel in the valley, rolling easy and open across an empty, empty sky, and the ridges drawn back, reverent of it. She has seen very few black people. Shell was one of the first. She caught Lil staring and shut the kitchen door in her face, but it had a glass window in it and she could still watch Shell, at least she could watch the color of her, wavy behind the door like sunken in water. Then Lucy carried out to her the leavings of a pie crust baked into little wafers. Lucy moving in all four places, shoulders, elbows, hips, knees, it seems like a ghost girl when Lil looks back now, like a spirit when she sees Lucy in her mind move like that, beautiful Lucy. Pap sat away across the pasture on the edge of the place, squatting under a hickory tree, waiting. Wouldn't get too near the house. Like a cat not petted as a kitten that way.

That ole rock pile is bound to be snaky in the summer, Lucy is saying, the sooner we get up there the better. They'll still be sluggy this time of year.

Cash money I don't have much use for, Lil says.

She didn't intend to say it. It's just what comes out of her mouth because she's too tired to catch it. But Lucy stiffens across the bed, and now she knows she's in trouble.

Cause you're ig'nernt, Lucy spits. Ain't been out of these hills longer'n fourteen minutes in all your fourteen years, what would you know about cash money? You and your babified notions and your sun in the ground and doing God knows what to yourself out in that shed.

Then Lucy bulls there in the dark, and Lil tries to stay awake and agree to it (*but for the grace*), but she feels her mind following her body away. Lucy snatches the sore muscle in her arm and squeezes.

Money's not all's in that cave. She waits, but Lil says nothing back.

If the sun goes in the mountain like you believe it does, don't you think it'll have to pass through that big hollowed-out place in the cave? In there, I bet you can see it up close. Where else would the heat in the warming dens come from? We'll spend the night and find out.

Lil's heart sits up despite itself, reaches out a little paw. And it cups that notion, gentle.

* * *

The way to the Club the cart cannot pass over. You have to travel the flank of the mountain they call Washboard, all the little ridges running down off it. Lil goes alone except for three rabbits bouncing in the bloodied sack that she will get cash for to bring back to Lucy.

She moves easy along that Washboard path using the sides of her feet. And free of the cart rattle behind her back, for a while, it's like it used to be for her in the woods. Everything coming all at once with no gap between its leaving where it is and its reaching her, the press of the hills up around her hips, and her, her moving. Coasting fallen logs and greenbrier clumps, nimble quick and never trip, how you can do it when you don't throw the thinking up to mess you, and the sun rocking along overhead with her. Whirring. And always just behind her, curling out of the edges of her eyes, the little spirits that, if she turns and tries to see them straight on, throw up their arms and swallow themselves.

Then a few rocks tumble out under her feet. It's not that they make her stumble. They don't. But the rumble of them recalls the cart, so it all stops, and the space rushes back in between her and the land. Her feeling everything a couple seconds late and what it loses in those couple seconds.

She takes a fork to an outcrop where she catches her breath, and from up above, the Club is a storybook kind of thing. Set there in a pretty hollow, broad, Lord it is a broad place, and open all the way down to the river with a good creek curving through it. The Club is for rich people, millionaires, some say. They come in the fall to hunt and the spring to fish, and for a long time, before she had ever been there, she believed the rich people just came up from town. When she was younger, and her thoughts couldn't reach any further than that. But Lucy said no. She said they were people from Outside, rode the train in from far away, came in all the way from Baltimore and Washington, Pittsburgh, Philadelphia (a lovely name, a name with fish swimming in it). The Washboard path drops down at the mouth of the hollow back behind the outbuildings. On her way to the kitchen, she passes the big garden with the boy in it today, working up the ground to plant.

After that, she walks slower. Because from up close, the Club works on her rough. Rubs her away, her muscles and her face and her hair and her strong teeth. Until nothing's left but the kind of skin dirt Mom calls rust. Lil just a scum of rust hovering and three dead bunnies in a bloodied sack.

A dying grease smell wobbles around the kitchen porch. She bangs on the screen door for some time, but no one answers, so she tries the handle, just a wee little bit so if someone is in there they won't notice, but it is hooked from the inside. She turns and sits on the edge of the front porch, the sack beside her, damp. Gamey-smelling. Crawling a little with the parasites. It is the cook Lil has to deal with although she hates it, the cook dammed up in her face like she is. All of what she has ever thought of saying stored up in the back of her mind where she'll only lose a sliver like striking a chip off a log. From somewhere in the Club a clock chimes (things are done on time in the valley, Lucy says, done by the clock, begin fixing supper at four, feed at five, eat at six, bed at nine, it's good to have a system, she says). Once she went to Keadles to fetch Lucy when Pap got into one of his bad ways and Mrs. Keadle told her to wait. She wandered out under a water maple and she waited. She started waiting with the sun striking straight down and she was waiting with it nudging the ridge. She was waiting when Mr. Keadle went to feed, and she saw him, but he didn't see her. She was waiting when Mr. and Mrs. Keadle came out to sit on the porch after supper. Why, what are you doing here? Them laughing. Why, why didn't you remind me? Time. The sun in this branch the sycamore. The sun in the next.

She walks back to the screen door and crushes her face against it. It was a long haul over the side of Washboard to find the cook gone, and the rabbits won't keep. She knows she'll have to talk to the boy.

He, too, makes her wait for quite a spell by the side of the garden before he barefoots across the broken soil moving about as fast as Pap on a bad day. He holds several more years than she does behind that stone-boned face, his face shaped like it has the crooked chunks of limestone under it, but he is no taller than her and looks to be less strong.

"You know where the cook's at?" she asks.

He gazes at her, not friendly. For a while, she thinks he won't answer. Some minutes pass, and she can see his eyes, but she doesn't see anything working. He is like a horse that way, she realizes later. A dog is different, shows it in the eyes before it turns mean, but often times a horse will not.

"Reckon to find her today you'll have to go through the front."

She looks over her shoulder in that direction. She's only studied the front from up above in the woods. A deep porch running the length of it, and the porch peppered with the baby rocking chairs, and on the lawn a few horses tethered to cast-iron hitching posts shaped like (she knows because Lucy has told her) horses tethered. Outside people no bigger than grasshoppers creep up and down doing whatever it is they do. And from up there she could blot out the whole porch just by raising her arm.

"Where in the front?" she asks.

He takes his time answering this one, too. "Just go on in the front door and ask at the desk."

The cottontails hang heavy in their sack (the heaviness a dead thing will make, so much lighter live, as though even when the live thing is not touching ground, not touching anything, it is still bearing itself on the air). She doesn't trust the boy, and she wants worse than anything else to drop the rabbits and head for home, but Lucy *(but for the grace)* will never forgive her if she comes back without her cash money.

She tries the kitchen door again before she does what he says. Then she stops and she closes her eyes and she prays. Prays they won't be able to see her, but nothing warm follows the prayer and she knows it was not heard. She makes an arc out through that open, open front lawn so she can cross the porch straight to the door and not have to pass the length of it.

There are three of them on the porch, and all are men. Her a floating scum of rust ruddered by enormous bare feet. Even though she's seen pictures of them (in Lucy's books, her magazines), even though she's seen them from a distance and even a few up close pass fast on a horse, she had no idea about the smell. The politely dead smell of them. Not an animal dead, but a flowery one, a sinking and smothering, rotten crushed honeysuckle, ringing them like they are polished stones dropped in this pool of odor.

She doesn't know which one it was done it. This is why she is stung that one of them knows her. They say nothing until she passes, no. They wait and say it behind her back.

"That's the sister," one says.

"Sister of who?" says another.

"Sister of that doe Fairlane got last fall."

Then she does look at them. Two youngish sleek-faced ones, rich-man fat in their bodies but their faces unworried as children's. Kind of snickering like they know they should not, and they stop that quick when she turns around. But there is a third, a heavy older one who looks sick in the face. A blunt sick like the fire-scarred butt of a tree. And this one looks away before she does.

* * *

At first she thinks the Rileys' place is empty, that all of them are off to strip bark. Then when she stops to draw breath, the granny shapens out of the dim way back under the eaves of the front porch. The granny calls to them, trilling, faint, like a little baby calling you. She has lost her mind, and they say she is all the time looking for it. Hullo, Mrs. Riley, Lil calls back in hopes of keeping her away, her pull-

ing the cart over the beat-down ground between the Rileys'
house and their sheds. The granny shadows them, hugging
the wall of the house with one shoulder. In her arms she
carries the muskrat hide she strokes deep-fingered like it is
a puppy. She stops when she reaches the back porch, her
head tilted. One side her face rubbed in the muskrat fur,
the other side eyeing them.

They coast on down to the sometimes creek, a puny
draught of water butting its head through rocks even
though this is April. And that is the bottom of Lockenjer.
Lil doesn't see a path, and she looks up for the top, but it is
only benches she sees. Trick tops, they will fool you. Hit a
bench and believe you're almost there, and then you lift
your face to see several more above it. She turns around to
Lucy folded up in the cart. Lucy, glimmering there from the
waist up, even Lil can see that, and all the tree branches
straining to make their little leaves come on.

Straight up, Lucy says, that's how Shell told it.

Lil leans into the harness. The best way to go would be a
Z, but the cart won't turn that tight. She settles for a loose
S until the cart slips anyway and nearly spills Lucy because
its wheels can't grip in the dead leaves. So she'll have to
haul it straight up. *Like Shell told it,* she guesses. Lil prays
and doesn't wait for the Lord having heard it.

She can only pull for ten steps, she counts them, before
she has to stop and tamp down the burn in her lungs. But
then it is terrible on her back just to hold the cart hanging
there, so she has to sweet-talk it, coddle and coax it, apol-
ogize, beg. She thinks of the sold horse, Bob. The switch on
his rump when Pap thought he was lazy. Back behind her
in the cart, Lucy takes to singing some song Lil's never
heard, something she must have picked up at Keadles.
Sings whiskery and under her breath, the tune slipping out
only now and again in little gouts as though she is far, far

away from Lil and singing with her head turned in a hard wind. Lil stops again and raises up to straighten her back. The dogwood makes a Christ on the cross, multiplies it by a million.

At last she reaches the first bench. She makes herself take her time wrestling the cart to a level place where it can't get away from her before she wiggles out of the harness and bends down in the dead leaves. She lays for a long time with no thoughts except, flickering a little, the maybe of the sun wheeling through the cave that night. Lucy stops singing. Says, Well, we better get moving.

She drags the wagon to the bottom of the next rise, grunts into the harness, and pulls until tears fill her eyes because this one is even steeper than the last. She pulls and she pulls and she counts her steps until the counting place in her head goes red and black, Lucy singing, whispery, her voice frayed out in this moany sigh, and Lil pulls and she counts again, and she's on seven when it happens. The harness (old Bob's tack, that tired, tired leather, older even than old Bob for all Lil knows, Pap working over it in the winter, rubbing the grease into it, fashioning it for her and him not good at that kind of thing, he did the best that he could, and Lil having sweated into it, leaked pus into it, bled into it just a little bit, and having pulled into it until she has begun to take on her the old Bob smell that is sunk into it), the harness snaps in two. She whips around reaching for the cart but misses before it plunges into a steep drop where two folds of the mountain make a shallow gully glutted with dead leaves. It dumps Lucy halfway down, and then spills the bedding and food they had for the night in the cave, and then it takes to traveling end over end until it crashes into a rock nearly big as a privy and smacks up into a dozen pieces.

Lil looks back to where it left Lucy in the leaves layered

there. She is on her stomach, arched in the small of her back, lifted, her head waving back and forth. Snail feelers, Lil thinks of. Moving down there like a snake with knuckles. Then she is ashamed. Lil skids down to where Lucy lies. But there is not much left on Lucy to hurt, and she is not hurt new.

First Lil tries the Rileys, just in case some of them might have come back early, because she knows they have a mule. As she climbs out of the creek bed, she sees the granny, poking round and round the house in a ring, one shoulder grating along the wall, the other hand dangling the muskrat hide in the dirt. Lil hollers at the house for some time, but no one comes out, and she knows she'll have to cross that granny's ring. She waits 'til the granny's disappeared around a corner, then she holds her breath, and leaps over the round-the-house rut in the ground. While she pounds at the door, she stays leery of her, listening close for her to make her round. But then she leaves her mind off the granny for a second to think how she'll have to carry Lucy out on her back. And when Lil turns around, there she is. The granny. Has creeped right up on her without noise, and huddles there. Her face as old as the meat in a walnut and the urine stink hovering her like a haunt, and she says, she says to Lil, "A bird in the bush is worth two in the hand."

*   *   *

The day after, it rains. Lil lies in the shed, the Bible window sealed like a scab on the air. And it comes to her that she is younger and dumber and uglier, but also not really stronger. Lucy in the back of the house with her magazines, her books, the pictures. Lil looks up at the Bible window and scares herself with understand. She knows what it is, for a minute, to grow out of these hills. The space forever between its quitting where it is and its reaching her. And yet she understands that to grow out and to leave out are two very different things.

The bullet only has to strike the right place, no bigger than your thumb, and like a key in a lock, it shuts down everything below. She had never known that before last fall. November, a nasty rain with grit in it, and Lil and Mom walking the woods, calling Lucy's name, and they passed near her twice before they heard her mewl back.

This rain leaks loud in a nail keg. Lil hoists her skirt up over her waist. She lifts her legs at the hips, and they come along heavy as andirons. She peers for the muscle, the bone. But with the way the dim lays up in the shed and some odd way a little light struggles in it, what she sees most clearly along her legs is an even coat of fine black hair.

She drops her legs in the dirt. And as her heels hit the ground, she thinks she hears old Bob blow.

She feels outside the shed the *there* you can catch off a big animal even when you cannot see it. She rolls onto her feet and tiptoes to the door of the shed in time to spy the rump of a black horse moving through the warm and heavy rain. A black mare so big she can hear over top the water stoning the shed roof the slocking her hoofs make in the lot mud, and she is so taken with what she can feel is balled up under that black hide, only after the mare stops at the porch does Lil notice she is mounted by a man tented over in oilskins and wearing a hat that makes a funnel.

Out onto the front porch hobbles Pap, wary, slow, sticking close the open door. Lil slips across the lot, gliding light so as not to draw attention. Rain pounding and runneling straight off the gutterless roof to drive into the ground, and she ducks through a sheet of it and tucks up under an eave to where she can see both Pap and the rider and smell the live fresh odor rising off the black mare in a steam. Finally Lil looks up to the hat pouring water off the nape of the man's neck like a funnel and she sees it is him. The Outside man with the blunt sick in his face, and somehow Pap already knows who it is although she didn't until the day on the Club porch.

Lil remembers his body under the oilskins. Not loose and saggy, but filling his clothes like a meal sack. Prick a hole and watch it dribble out. Packed like that. "I've come to make a gesture at restitution," the Outside man says, snipping every syllable short.

Pap says nothing back. He stands there curved a little along his backbone with his arms forked out from his body and his hands hanging open and loose like he's ready to fight. Or to run.

The Outside man's hands vanish into the oilskins. When he pulls from a secret place a bundle of bills, the mare shifts her great weight from one hip to the other. "It was an accident, of course," he says. A pair of scissors he carries in his mouth.

Pap does not move. Now Lil sees that Mom is filling the doorway behind Pap with her hammy arms up either side the frame. The only place she shows her feelings is in her bare feet, toes clenching the porch floor. Mom speaks. "We're not innerested in your cash money," she says.

The mare throws her head, just the little she can with the tight rein he has her under. She bares her teeth in the bit, working at it with the back of her tongue. Then, just when everything, everyone, seems locked up tight, a voice from behind Mom, very clear even over top the rain, opens it all up again.

"Take it, Pap."

Pap seems not to have heard. As Lil stands there swallowing up that mare, she feels a rushing back inside her. Lucy calls again, a little closer than before.

"Take it, Pap."

Then Mom is stumbling aside, Lucy butting at her hip, and Lucy knuckles her way out onto the porch. Rain driving into the dirt, and the horse a wondrous heat just being there, and Lucy using the top of herself to drag the bottom of herself out onto the porch, and then slowly, gracefully, glimmery Lucy, she pulls her bottom half around like it is a bolt of hair she is arranging, and she places it underneath her in a lovely heap. Then, polite, she holds out one hand for the money.

The Outside man stands in his stirrups, and then he starts to swing his leg over the mare's behind. But he is awkward in the oilskins, and he gets hung up, his heel tangled somewhere. His hat like a funnel spills its water the wrong way, down his sleeve. He gives up and settles back in the saddle. He motions to Pap to come get it, but Pap won't move. So the Outside man tosses the bundle of bills underhand to Lucy.

The cash drops off to the side of her legs, but Lucy snatches it up quick like something striking.

Lil moves back into the rain to where she can watch the horse leave. And it is a beautiful thing, if you have seen it, to watch a heavy horse travel down a steep hill in the rain. Bunch-muscled in the rump and the tight flesh shuddering from side to side. Slipping hard under the skin, and the great thrust and plunge forward checked suddenly when she locks her knee. Muscle against muscle. But still moving. Lil stands and watches, not minding the rain. Not even minding when the mare disappears in the black trees. She's given the liveness in the horse.